Also by Ray Ordorica

The Alaskan Retreater's Notebook
Border Caper
Casablanca Caper
Sixty Years of Testing Guns

CARACAS CAPER

by
Ray Ordorica

Cover photo "Four-Inch Nickel M29"
and cover design by Ray Ordorica

ISBN: 978-1-7331352-1-4

SHEEP CREEK PUBLISHING
NORTH FORK, IDAHO

This book is dedicated to my very
patient kids, Homer and Louie

This is a work of fiction. Other than a few real persons mentioned, all the characters in this book are fictitious. Any similarity to persons living or dead is purely coincidental and unintentional. Once again, if your name closely resembles any of the characters in this book, you have our deepest sympathy.

TABLE OF CONTENTS

CHAPTER 1
Victims

A piercing scream shattered the serenity of the mid-summer morning, scaring the songbirds to silence. Harsh and high-pitched — the cry of a mountain lion? — the scream came from within the dense woods that lined the east side of the river along which two men were canoeing. It came again. This time a shouted word ruled out cougar and ruled in human. "No! **NO!**" and then a brief scream overridden by three shots. The two men paddling the old Grumman canoe down the river, deep in Idaho's back country, froze at the sound of gunfire.

The men didn't speak. The man in front pointed at the shore, and together they drove the canoe up onto a sandy spot, got out and pulled it up out of the reach of the swift stream. The man in front secured it by its painter to a handy young pine.

They looked at each other for a few seconds in silence. One man spoke.

"You want to take point, Rico?"

"No, but I will," said Ricardo Henry Morgan, private investigator.

His closest friend, frequent work associate and Mexican expatriate Modesto Pincata Buena, aka Mole, said, "We may be here a while. Let's get our stuff outa the canoe and stash it, just in case it rains."

"Good idea."

The men brought their knapsacks and sleeping bags out of the canoe and hid them in the thick brush some thirty yards from the canoe. They covered the pile with a camo tarp. With a hard look at the terrain visible across the river from the landing, Rico spoke. "Mole, take a good look across at that rock formation across the river. We need to make sure we can find our way back here."

"Already done, *amigo. ¡Vamos!*"

They plunged into the deep woods, Rico in the lead, his nickel-plated four-inch Model 29 Smith & Wesson 44 Magnum sixgun in hand, following a compass direction east of the river. Mole was ten yards behind him, carefully keeping his Robar NP3'ed 40-caliber Browning Hi-Power pointed away from Rico's back. Their eyes scanning everything they could see, the two men pressed cautiously on toward where they thought the sound had come from. From time to time Rico stopped and looked back the way he came, making sure he could find his way out of the dense forest. It was not easy to pass quietly through the thick brush under the trees, and they made some unavoidable noise.

Rico stopped after they had gone about a hundred yards. When Mole came up, Rico asked in a near whisper, "Am I going in the right direction? Whadda ya think?"

"Try a bit off to the left. Can't see much, but I think there's a lighter area over there, maybe fewer trees and we can get a better idea of what's going on."

Another few minutes' thrashing through the undergrowth brought the men to the edge of a clear area a hundred yards across and nearly as wide. To the east side of the clearing the terrain rose in a concave crag fifty or more yards high. The rest of the area behind the crag and to the sides of the clearing was covered with more thick trees like those through which the men had come. The base of the clear area was flat rock, a natural formation that prevented trees and other brush from growing there. Behind the crag the mountains rose steep and rugged, thickly covered in pine.

"This could be a helipad," said Mole. "But no helicopter in sight."

"It's a natural amphitheater. That crag reflected the sounds. That's why we heard the screams and shots so well in the river."

"What's that on the south side?" Mole pointed.

A flap of something of an odd color moved in the light breeze in the clearing, just beyond a slight rise in the ground. The men made their way carefully and silently under the cover of the trees in that direction. They found them just outside the edge of the woods. Three bodies lay there on the bare earth close to each other, the blood oozing from them seeping into cracks in the rocks and going home into the ground. Each body had a bullet hole in its forehead. They had once been a woman and two men, but now were just discarded things no one wanted any more.

"See anyone?" Rico spoke first, quietly, still within the cover of the trees.

"Not yet. Lemme get over to that crag and climb up a bit and have a look-see."

"Good idea, but wait 'til I get up this tree so I can keep an eye on you."

Rico climbed until he was ten feet off the ground, made himself secure, cleared a few branches out of his view, and nodded to Mole.

Mole quickly made his way around the south side of the clearing over to the base of the crag, staying well within the cover of the trees. The crag's base consisted of large chips, chunks and boulders fallen from the rock face a thousand years ago, now nicely settled into a terrace snugly up against the base of the big rock that made climbing easy. Mole went up the boulder stair-steps to a ledge that gave him a good view of the clearing. Once secure on the small ledge he scanned the surrounding country as far as he could see. He saw nothing but trees and more trees in the wilderness. He rejoined Rico. "Nothin'."

"Okay, now let's take a look at these guys."

They began a careful examination of the dead trio, not moving anything more than necessary. As they began, Mole said, "Rico, I've seen that woman's face somewhere. Isn't she famous or something?"

"She doesn't look familiar to me, but this fellow in the suit sure is." The dead man wore a dark-blue suit of good cloth with white shirt, vest and red tie, and polished, nearly new oxfords. "He's Jimmy Fleetwing. He used to star in that old TV show, *Busting Ground*. He was in a coupla movies recently, too. Isn't this him?"

"Yeh, you're right. What the frap was a Hollywood actor doing out here? And now I know this woman. She's Molly Fender, hostess of the TV interview show, *Fun For Your Life*." She wore a pleated dark-green skirt of knee length, flat-heel dress shoes and a loose light-green blouse. Her long dark hair hung loose.

"Mole, you've got it. I saw an episode of it once when Sally wanted to watch an interview with some up-and-coming fiddler. Molly Fender did the interview. How about this third guy? Who's he?"

The third object was dressed in ripped-at-the-knee faded jeans, a worn green and red checkered shirt, a loose-fitting and

4

somewhat dirty old brown leather jacket, and ancient, scuffed hiking boots.

"Rico, this woman and the first guy look like they could walk onto a TV set with the clothes they're wearing, but Contestant Number Three looks like he'd be right at home in some dark alley among the street people in 'Frisco. Whadda ya theenk." Mole's Mexican street accent slipped into the discussion.

"I 'theenk' it's time, ol' buddy, to do the digging and see if they have any ID on 'em. Then, somehow, we've got to report this...to someone." Rico bent to the task.

A brief inspection of the wallet of the well-dressed man and the woman's small clutch proved them to be the people the men had guessed them to be. The third man had no wallet, no identification at all.

"Rico, your actor here's wearing a Rolex watch and there's several hundred dollars in his wallet and also a couple credit cards. So whatever it was, this wasn't a robbery."

"Mole, I think all we can do is continue downstream and report this. We could look around the woods for the shooter, but I suspect he's gone, or at least gone into hiding waiting for a ride outa here. Let's make for the canoe."

Half an hour later Rico and Modesto were back on the shore of the river where they had left the old Grumman canoe. The canoe was gone.

"*Pues, amigo*, good idea we took our packs outa the canoe. Looks like the shooter stole our ride." Mole cursed and spat into the river. "So what's next, *Pobrecito*? Wanna go swimming?"

Rico said, "Man, Paul's gonna be pissed. After all the hassle we gave him before he flew us in with his old canoe. Now we've lost the damned thing." Rico's friend Paul Gobbarander owned a helicopter service and also owned the old Grumman canoe. It took a lot of coaxing by Rico to persuade Paul to fly the two men and the canoe, strapped to the skids, into the wilds of Idaho's back country and put them down near the head of the river. Their plan was to canoe down the stream for a week or ten days, camping out and relaxing to get rid of the stress remaining in the wake of their recent great battle with nasty international politicians. They would eventually come out to the town of North Bedford in western Idaho, where the stream they were on joined with the Rickaree river. Rico parked his old Dodge Stealth R/T Twin Turbo at North Bedford, and when they arrived back at the town they'd return the canoe to Paul and drive home to the other side of the state where Rico lived. "Paul really liked that old canoe. We can't replace it."

"Well, *amigo*, whoever stole it is going exactly where we were going, so we can look for it once we get outa here. The big problem seems to be, how do we get outa here?" Mole thought they were stymied.

"Don't worry about that. Paul gave me an emergency satellite-messenger device. I've got it in my pack, so we can always use that. But I think there's an easier way out. The dead guys and whoever shot them must've been brought in here by chopper. They couldn't walk in here, and the killer couldn't have counted on our coming along to give him a canoe ride. The two Hollywood types haven't been in here long, not with those clothes. So I'm guessing the helicopter will come back...."

"Unless the killer radioed to cancel the ride." Mole completed Rico's thoughts.

"He must've seen us or heard us," replied Rico, "and figured the only way for us to get here was by boat. So he figured that'd be the fastest and safest way outa here, 'cause he must've

6

figured we heard the shots and were coming to investigate. He couldn't afford to stick around for his ride."

Mole answered, "How about we make camp by the clearing before we try Paul's satellite messenger, and see if someone comes. If they do come it'll probably be late this evening."

And that is what they did, setting up a simple lean-to shelter within the trees near the clearing.

Just before nightfall, in the last good light of the day, Mole said, "Here she comes!"

"Eh?"

"I hear a chopper."

"Good ears," said Rico. I can't hear it yet."

Within a few minutes a helicopter began to settle into the clearing. The two men stayed out of sight to see what it would do. The chopper hovered at treetop level, turned nearly a full circle, and then departed without touching the ground.

"Well, *amigo*," said Rico, "looks like we didn't know the right signal to get him to land."

"I got the N number, but chances are this bird was just hired by someone to bring these folks here. The bodies are visible to him, so maybe he got scared off."

"It's time to use our satellite messenger, ol' buddy. We better ask Paul to bring along the local sheriff." Rico walked back to their lean-to. He sent the satellite message and then the two men made a comfortable camp for the night and waited for the morning delivery of the lawman.

CHAPTER 2
Lando

"**W**ell, the goddamn canoe is here in town somewhere. Has to be. He had no reason to take it any further than the junction. It gets damned dangerous to go any further downstream." Rico Morgan was in his thirties, slim, tall and tough. He looked like a cross between James Coburn and Chuck Norris, but without Chuck's bulk. His sandy hair was already going gray. A week's worth of beard clouded his normally clean-shaven face. Rico sat in a straight chair in the sheriff's outer office. Sheriff Carl Lutz was there with Rico and Paul Gobbarander, with Mole leaning against the wall in the background, listening to Rico's rant.

The previous evening Paul received notice from the GEOS center in Houston minutes after Rico and Mole sent the rescue call with the satellite messenger. Paul contacted the sheriff, who got a forensics man and photographer to meet him and Paul at the little heliport early the next morning. Paul flew them out to pick up Rico, Mole, their gear, and the three bodies. Forensics documented the murder scene with photos, videos and notes. They then loaded the bodies, and Paul flew them all out. They were still with the sheriff that afternoon at his office.

"So where's my friggin' canoe? You gonna pay for it?" Paul, an ex-Marine with a short, stocky and powerful body, was furious with Rico Morgan.

"Whyn't you guys put a cork in it." Sheriff Lutz said, with a marked look of disgust. "You'll either find the canoe or you won't. If he can't find it, Morgan will reimburse you, Paul, like he said he would. We have more important things in front of us, gentlemen. Who the hell's this third guy? He looks like a bum, except he's got clean fingernails and he's in great shape physically under the rags. He sure ain't a homeless bum."

Rico folded his arms across his chest. His dark blue cotton shirt stunk, he noticed, from three days of wear. His other shirt in his pack was even worse. "Nothing on prints yet?"

"No, spoke the sheriff. "Morgan, you've got some sort of a reputation for finding trouble. What's your take on this? Any ideas? I mean we've got a TV reporter, a movie star, and somebody else."

"I have none. We heard screams, shots, went to look, and found what you saw there."

"And there was no sign of anyone leaving? You didn't see anyone?"

"That's why we lost the canoe. We didn't see a bloomin' thing. And we didn't just go waltzing in there making noise like it was a parade."

Mole was standing against the wall with his arms crossed, blending in unseen and unheard, something he was quite good at, even though he wore a red and black checkered wool shirt and a black military-style floppy campaign hat. He was in his late thirties, had a black beard, and was fit as a fiddle. So far he had said nothing. He broke his silence. "When you expect something from the prints?"

The sheriff looked at him as though the wall had spoken. Regaining his composure he replied, "Actually we thought we'd know by now, but it looks like tomorrow at best. Prob'ly not this afternoon."

Rico leaned back in the chair, rocking it onto its back legs. "Sheriff, how about my friend and I go see if we can find Paul's canoe. We'll check with you tomorrow. We're staying right down the street."

"Yeah, okay. I've got your statements. Might as well do something useful. See you tomorrow." The sheriff walked into his office and the three men filed out into the afternoon sunshine.

Paul said, "Rico, Mole, I know you guys didn't do this on purpose, but please see if you can find the damned thing. I've had it over thirty years. It's part of me. You know how that goes." With a wave of his burly hand he broke off from the other two. Rico and Mole drove to the small hotel and checked in, and then went to scour the riverside and any local landing areas to see if the ancient Grumman was there.

Later that afternoon Rico phoned his girlfriend Sally Foarth from the hotel room. "Sally, we're off the river but we won't be back right away."

"Zounds, Rico, you're outa the woods too soon. Didn't expect to hear from you for another week. What gives?"

"Zounds? Hmmm. What have you been reading? We, er, hit a snag and we have to stay in North Bedford for a day or so. We had an emergency and got Paul to fly us out."

"What'd you break? Leg? Arm? Ass?"

"None of the above. We, er, got involved in a triple murder, and..."

"Goddamn it Rico! Can't you stay out of trouble when you're supposed to be having a good time camping, canoeing, living the wild life? Three murders? Asshole!"

"Not our fault, dearest. We were just in the right place to hear something go down, took a look, and found a bunch of dead people. And then someone stole our canoe."

"Jesus! Always something! Tell me about it." Sally tried to simmer down, but Rico could tell she was still ready to blame him for the shooting.

"You recall that interview of a fiddle-guy? Done by Molly Fender on *Fun For Your Life* a few months back?"

"Yes, of course. I taped it and watched it several times."

"Molly's dead."

"What!"

"So's Jimmy Fleetwing from *Busting Ground.* "

"Rico, what the hell's going on!? Wait. You said three victims. Who's number three, the President?"

"We don't know who he is. Dressed like a bum. No ID."

"Can you tell me more? How'd you guys get involved?"

Rico filled Sally in on the story.

"So we'll be here a few days yet. Hopefully the sheriff will have some clue about this in a day or two and then — maybe even before that — we can come home."

"Good luck finding Paul's canoe. Call me."

Rico Morgan leaned back, nodded to Mole, and grabbed his beer. The beer was Mirror Pond Pale Ale, one of Rico's favorites. The two men sat together in the hotel room awhile, neither saying anything. Finally Rico broke the silence. "Mole, let's go get some dinner, and then do some more canoe lookin'. I saw a Chinese place down the street."

"Pues, amigo, I wonder if there's the chance of the smell of money for Rico Morgan and Company in this mess." Mole downed the last of his beer, rose and grabbed his jacket.

————————

Rico Morgan was a private eye of a different sort. Instead of checking up on errant spouses with a clandestine camera he catered to high-dollar clients of his own choosing. Rico set up a group of five part-time people to search the Internet and other news sources, monitor street talk, and keep an eye on other international groups for problems that fell into the realm of what he and his team could solve.

The group, called Boise Control, consisted in five people of diverse backgrounds. The unofficial head of the group was I. Yeats Prunzalot, a computer-hacking genius.

Another member was George William (G. Willie) Kers, a retired Chrysler executive who had traveled the world and had contacts everywhere.

Then there was Myrtle Stockwood, an ex-hooker now in her sixties who knew people and could dig into their psyche better than most shrinks, and do it in a heartbeat.

Eileen Tudarite, an ex-Wall Street trader with excellent financial gains from her online trading securely deposited in her bank account, was friends with President Trump. She had vast knowledge of international money affairs and many connections.

The youngest member of Boise Control was the Dutch girl Kikkan DaKrotch, whose knowledge of world politics got her noticed by the Nobel people, by Alex Jones, and finally by Rico Morgan.

Together the team worked to find suitable tasks for Rico and sometimes Mole. Once Rico said "Go" the team did background work and research on the problem for Rico and then turned him loose on the generally difficult and usually dangerous job.

Occasionally a potential client would contact Boise Control and ask them to get involved. That happened on the last job Rico took on. It was an investigation into illicit border crossings and murder, the job funded by Immigration & Customs Enforcement, commonly called ICE, through its parent office, Department of Homeland Security. ICE contacted Rico's group in Boise, Idaho, about the problem. The story was written up in *Border Caper*.

Rico Morgan lived with two cats in an old frame house on a small ranch some distance north of Salmon, Idaho, near some of the roughest, toughest mountain terrain in the United States. His friend Modesto Pincata Buena, whom Rico called Mole, was born in Mexico but was now a U.S. citizen who lived in New Mexico in the desert off the beaten track, not far from Las Cruces. Despite their individual preferences for hot and cold home climates, the two men had experienced many adventures together for a long time. Alone or in the company of their ladies the two men had hunted, fished, camped, fought, flown, drank, laughed, cried, and nearly died many times together. They enjoyed the outdoors and everything it offered.

Some years ago Mole's wife died and he never remarried. He told Rico he was threatening to get a new girlfriend, but so far no one was a steady companion to the rugged Mexican man.

Rico's lady was Sally Foarth, a world-renowned concert violinist and a prodigy since her childhood on the instrument. Now in her late twenties, she often traveled the world on tour with her loaner Guarneri del Gesu violin, so her time together with Rico was on the rare side, and thus vastly enjoyed by both of them. Sally was about a decade younger than Rico, an age difference that meant nothing to either of them. She had a house not far from Rico's little ranch, so when she was not touring it was easy for them to get together. Rico played banjo, guitar and mandolin, and was trying desperately to learn violin. Though he was not in the same class as Sally that didn't stop them from playing duets together. And so they had fun, and time moved along at its usual merry pace.

———————

Rico ate his pork-fried rice with a fork while Mole used chopsticks. "Mole, I can't imagine how this triple murder can get us any money. We don't know why three people were killed. Maybe something was stolen, or someone had knowledge they ought not to have had. Let's say a gold brick was stolen. Why did three non-related people have to die? Could they identify the crook? Sure, but if the crook got away, with or without our canoe, he could just disappear and wouldn't have to face a murder rap when he's caught."

"Unless these three knew him well, and could easily find him. Dead men tell no tales. Still, like you I don't see the need to kill 'em. But do we know they were unrelated? Why not have your people do some digging on this? See if anything pops. Maybe the two TV people were in some deal together."

"Good call," replied Rico. "I'll contact Yeats first thing tomorrow and gave him the names. See what he can dig out. So what do we do about the canoe? Any idea where it might be?"

"We can look along the river to the north end. We checked the south pretty well this afternoon."

After their dinner the men walked the shoreline for several hours but found exactly nothing that looked like a canoe. They did find an inviting bar, checked it out, had a beer apiece, and called it quits for the night.

The next morning there was a phone message at the hotel for Rico. He dialed the number and it was the sheriff. "Hi, Sheriff, any news on the prints?"

Sheriff Lutz replied, "No, Morgan, but you're one lucky SOB. Some guy called from a mile below the main landing and said he found a drifting canoe. Grabbed it, and decided to call us instead of putting his own name on it. It's Paul's Grumman."

"Outstanding! Hell, I'll pay the guy a reward, or mebbe buy him a canoe of his own. Can I get his name?"

The sheriff gave it, and said, "I called Paul. He's on his way to get the canoe. Seemed kind of let down that he couldn't razz you any more about it."

"Thanks, Sheriff."

As soon as he hung up Rico got on the phone again to Boise Control. He dialed the direct line to I. Yeats Prunzalot, the unofficial head of the group. In his lingering Indian accent Yeats said, "Oh, ditty me, I was hoping it was you, kind sir, calling me on the phone on this bright and sunny day. I trust you are well?"

"Hi, Yeats, yes I am well and hope you are too. I have a bit of info to pass along to you about a problem here in the Idaho wilderness."

"Mr. Morgan, sir, is it about the dead TV person and the actor and other man who died recently there?"

Rico Morgan said to himself, "Holy crap! How the hell does he get this stuff, when it's either classified or brand-new or just plain damned obscure? I know he's a professional hacker, but...Jesus!" Out loud he said, "Good one, Mr. Prunzy. Yes indeed this request is about those three poor dead people. How, may I ask, did you hear about it?"

"Oh, Mr. Rico, I cannot tell you that precisely, except to say the information was on the hot airwaves and on the high-frequency radio lines yesterday if one were paying attention, and that is indeedy what you have me to do, is to pay attention."

"Okay, Yeats, sorry for asking. So what do you know about it? Or about them?"

"Other than the fact the woman and man who have been identified are both Canadian, I do not know much. I of course have their ages, professional information, home addresses, the usual things, but nothing much to point to as to why they were killed. I know that Molly Fender had a TV interview-type show, and the actor, former stage magician Jimmy Fleetwing, was in a few movies."

"Canadian?"

"Indeedy. In fact both were from the same small town some fifty miles out of Ottawa."

"Most interesting. Are they of the same age? Like, did they go to the same school?"

"The same school? That is most unlikely as he was ten years older than she. I am waiting on some potentially important information about a club or society they may both have been part of, but will not know for a few days yet."

"Okay, Yeats, thanks a bunch and please let me know if you find out anything more. I'll let you know if I find out who the third guy was."

Later that same morning the phone rang again in Rico's hotel room. Sheriff Lutz told him, "Morgan, we have a sort-of identity on the third guy."

"Hi, Sheriff. Whadda ya mean 'sort-of'?"

"The guy's name's Lando Canunny. Middle name Mel. His history goes back only six, maybe seven years. Before that there's nothing."

"Heck, that means he could be anyone. Is there any chance of a deeper search for his prints finding anything?"

"Possibly, if we don't get shut out by some goddamned government office. I mean if Canunny was an agent for one of the letter-boxes in DC, they won't tell us anything. Oops! I gotta go. Two guys just walked into my office and they look like they mean business. Black suits and all. What I just said, eh?"

"Sheriff, I'll be down there right away."

"Okay, Morgan."

Rico made a quick call to inform Yeats at Boise Control of the identity of the third body.

Half an hour later Rico and Mole walked into the sheriff's office where Sheriff Lutz was holding forth with two men in black suits. Their clipped-short haircuts told Rico just about all he needed to know before he or they said a word.

"Rico Morgan and, er, Mole," said the sheriff, "these guys are Billy Bledsome and Jack Marsters, and they're from Washington, DC, and they're here to tell us what to do and how to do it."

The two men in black were in their mid-thirties, and seemed to be in good physical condition. Rico noted, however, that neither had the gleam of intelligence in their eyes that ought to have been there if they were, in fact, top agents from any DC agency whatsoever. In short, he recognized them as potential goons.

"Gentlemen," spoke Rico, shaking hands with each. "So what does the CIA want us to do about this situation?"

Billy Bledsome had a prominent chin and narrow-set eyes. His dark short-cut hair was beginning to recede above a brow wrinkled with what appeared to be regret over not having a drink in his hand right then.

"Morgan," answered the man called Bledsome, "we never said we're from the CIA or any other agency, but our specific orders from DC are to instruct you and the good sheriff here to stay out of this investigation completely. It's a federal matter. We have men on the scene of the crime already, and will be taking this third victim back with us. We know you've been involved with international mysteries in the past, but please keep out of this one."

"I thought the official phrase was 'We can neither confirm nor deny we're CIA.' Are you slipping up? Or did you just forget?"

"Never mind. We want you to stay out of this. Got it?"

"I'll stay out of it, that is unless or until you guys give up and have to hire me. In that case, my group will charge your group only twice what we normally charge."

"Oh?" spoke Bledsome. "Why is that, supposing the unlikely event of that occurrence?"

"Gee, you talk just like you've been to Harvard. The reason is, I and my group don't like to be told what to do by amateurs. So if we get hired, which I admit is a strong possibility in this case, we'll have to do the natural thing and up our price."

"Why in hell do you think it's likely you'll be hired? Do you know something we don't?"

"Nope, not a thing. I just know you fellows are not always the best at investigating stuff like the murder of three people, two of whom you don't give a rat's ass about."

"Hold it, Morgan!" Jack Marsters finally opened his tight-lipped mouth. Marsters was shorter than Bledsome and quite slender, with black hair, a thin mouth and what appeared to be slightly more between his ears than Bledsome, judging by his somewhat more alert expression. "Whadda ya mean we don't care? We're going to look into this as deeply as we can. Where do you come off telling us we don't care about the other two dead people?"

"Well, first of all you called it an international mystery, but you didn't bother telling the sheriff here that the TV woman and the dead actor are in fact Canadians."

"What?" Sheriff Lutz was surprised.

Mole spoke. "Next, you didn't bother asking if the sheriff has notified next-of-kin of the other two, did you? Or if he'd made arrangements for the return of their bodies."

"No, they didn't," said the sheriff.

Mole spoke again. "So it's obvious you two turds care only why your agent got killed, and because of your search, ongoing now in the woods, your first priority is to try to recover whatever it was that was taken from the guy we think was one of your agents and the two show-biz Canadians."

The two CIA agents said nothing, and couldn't meet the eyes of anyone in the room.

Rico said, "Gentlemen, this stinks. Sheriff, we'll be going home now. You have my home phone number if you need to contact me, and we're only half a day's drive away."

"Right. Thanks, guys." He shook hands with Rico and Mole and they left his office.

As they walked back to the hotel, Mole said, "I bet your group gets hired within a week. These guys have stupid written all over themselves."

"I suspect you're right, buddy, but I sure do wonder what it was that was stolen. What was it doing there in the deep woods, and why did it take three people to carry it?"

"Yep, I agree," replied Mole, "it looks now like a sure thing something did get stolen. If it was just murder, why do these CIA goons have their people doing a search for something in the woods where the trio got killed?"

Rico added, "And why *did* the man and woman get killed? Mole, I think it's time to take a good look at the possibilities, once we get back home across the state."

"*¡Claro que sí!*"

CHAPTER 3
Suspicions

"Lando's missing!" Sally Foarth's section head Tom Dickannary spoke to her in the early morning from his office in DC. Sally was an agent of the NSA, which agency used her occasionally at her convenience on some of her world-wide violin-concert tours to gather information discretely. Not even her boyfriend Rico Morgan knew she was an agent.

"Lando Canunny, the CIA guy? Where'd he go missing, Tom?" The slim, dark-haired violinist had on her morning-at-home clothes, which was cutoffs, sandals, and a white blouse with no sleeves. The summer sun had given her skin a good tan. Her hair hung past her shoulders in a flowing, loose mop. Her blue eyes gazed out her kitchen window; she watched a robin dance on a branch of a tree growing close to her house.

"He's missing out of Venezuela. We know he was down there looking into the mechanics of the dissolution of that country. We overheard some gossip to the effect Canunny was supposedly talking with some top people in charge in Caracas. Sub-heads of state of the Maduro regime, for instance. Apparently quite a few of the higher-ups remain alive, coherent, and in control in Venezuela, which is an ongoing surprise for us. We were sure the other guy, Juan Guaidó, would be in charge by now, but Maduro has lots of clout and influence, way above what we thought he could muster. Anyway, Lando was part of a crew that was in Caracas supposedly finding out if anything tangible could be saved, or if not, then it was their job to deal with it properly, either pull it out of the country if it was mobile, like some of the top people, or maybe sabotage or destroy it so it can't be used against us, if it comes to either civil war or something worse.

"Some the higher-ups are pulling out, above and beyond all the, er, common people simply leaving. But as of last Tuesday Lando Canunny failed to make the requisite radio contact with his handler in Mexico. Lando hinted he was onto something big, but there's nothing more on it, whatever it was. Some of his people in the CIA think he was on a special trip and everything's okay, but there's no common agreement. He's basically missing."

"What sorts of things were they trying to salvage? Any idea?"

"Lando and the rest of the crew, maybe half a dozen guys or as many as a dozen, were there trying to get a handle on whatever military stuff they didn't want getting into bad hands, like weapons and some special Russia-inspired fighter aircraft. If the weapons couldn't be hidden or protected he was authorized by us to destroy them, if he could do so without the remaining military forces there stopping him. This was to try to prevent the start of World War Three. If there were no decent weapons remaining there, then the Maduro forces would not or could not strike effectively against either the starving natives armed with pitchforks, or any invading army that wanted to bring in food and medical supplies.

"The U.S. figured Venezuela was going down the tubes no matter who was in charge, so the CIA went there to poke around and see if they could do U.S. interests any good.

Canunny was part of the crew. He was also personally tasked with salvaging whatever financial stuff the country had that wasn't going to Turkey, and make offers to get the big stuff, like tons of gold, out of Venezuela to a favorable neutral country. Not Turkey. Certainly not Russia, nor Mexico nor half a dozen other Central and South-American countries.

"Lando Canunny was also supposed to see what could be done about the vast amount of crap sent there by the Russkies, and probably by Brazil as well. Find out what it was, what good it did, and what could be done about it. Most of the Russian stuff was weaponry of one sort or another. No surprise there.

"We also wanted to know if Mexico might have been wanting to send troops in to shore up Maduro's defenses because, although Mexico declares itself neutral, the truth is they still support the Maduro regime. But that's moot, now that Russia has sent troops there. That just happened, by the way, and you may not know about it.

"Bottom line, the U.S. wanted to get a better idea what exactly was going on in Caracas, so CIA sent a team there. They want to get a good handle on whoever is trying to shore up Venezuela and the Maduro regime against the hordes of starving natives who are starting to rise up, and against the potential usurper, that guy Guaidó. The Russians sent billions in support some time back, but other than lots of guns and other weapons we don't know exactly what the rest of it was. It could have been money, food, or maybe some technology. We know Lando helped a few of the dissident but top political dogs out by putting them, their families, and their belongings on one of the agency's carrier aircraft, a C-130. That was about a week ago. The plane has made a few other trips in and out, but Lando disappeared after the first flight."

"Okay, so you know Lando Canunny was in fact there. Could he have left with the evacuees?" Sally wondered.

"He could have, but wasn't supposed to. Long story short, if you hear anything about him, make contact." Tom cut the line.

Early the next day Rico phoned Sally from North Bedford and said they were on their way and would arrive mid-afternoon, so Sally dropped by Rico's house and opened up the windows to get fresh air circulating. She had been caring for Rico's two cats, Homer and Louie, while he was away, and the cats were glad to be home again. Later that day the cats tried their best to trip Rico and Mole as they came in dragging their camping packs with them. Rico grabbed beers for himself, Sally and Mole, and sprawled in his favorite chair. Homer, Rico's beautiful tabby, immediately jumped into his lap, dug in his claws, and purred audibly.

"Homer, I bet you want some beer, my friend. I know you've been at it while I was gone. And I know you've been into my cigars again. The beer and the cigars keep disappearing. I've heard you and Louie partying at four ayem, you little bum. Loud music, dancing, yowling, cavorting, and all the rest."

Homer gave a guilty purr.

"These guys have been into the Scotch, too," said Mole swaying back and forth on the rocking chair with the other cat, Louie, on his lap. "You can smell it on their breath!"

"You guys are remorseless," spoke Sally. "The poor cats behave themselves, you guys drink all the booze and smoke the stogies, and blame the cats. Shame on you!"

"Oh, no, Sally! They *do* drink the stuff. Watch this." Mole put his glass of beer near Louie's mouth. The huge, mostly white cat sniffed, said "No thank you!", bolted into the bedroom and hid under the bed.

"See how guilty he is?" Rico chuckled.

"Guilty my ass," said Sally. "Speaking of guilty, Roxy called you."

"Wha...why...f'ub, dabba?" Said Rico. His brief affair with Roxy some months in the past was, he hoped, unknown to Sally. At the time, Roxy Roades, a CIA agent, didn't know Sally was Rico's girlfriend, and Rico didn't know Roxy knew Sally. Rico and Roxy were lovers for a night, but when Roxy found out both of them knew Sally, Roxy called it off. Two ships passed in the night. Neither wanted to be torpedoed.

"She called me and told me she left a message for you. It oughta be on your phone recorder." Sally pretended to ignore the fumbling stammer of her boyfriend, but she noted his ears got slightly red.

"What the devil does she want?" Rico regained some of his composure.

"I suspect it's to do with the deaths. You might go listen to your recorder."

Eager for an excuse to leave the immediate presence of his lady friend, Rico got up, spilled a little beer, cursed under his breath and went to the kitchen, where the phone recorder resided.

Two messages were on it. The first was from Rico's old friend John Linebaugh. The message indicated Rico's new 500 Linebaugh revolver was ready to go and where should John ship it?

The second, from Roxy, was short. "Rico, the third man killed in Idaho was Lando Mel Canunny, one of our agents. Hope you're okay and out of the line of fire. Bye."

Rico opened another three bottles of beer and repaired to the great room where Mole was telling Sally about what they saw in the woods near the dead trio. Rico passed the beer bottles out and said, "That dead guy Lando is indeed CIA, which we suspected in North Bedford in the sheriff's office. That means the two goons there were in fact CIA, so what the hell's up? I wonder what else Roxy knows about the movements of Mr. Canunny."

The mention of Lando Canunny's name got Sally's attention, but she kept her interest hidden from the two men. She'd have to phone Tom Dickannary as soon as she could get away.

"Rico," said Sally, "I brought over a pot of beef stew I made yesterday. It's in the fridge, and enough for the both of you for maybe two days. There's some tilapia and a couple steaks in the freezer, and a few fresh potatoes and carrots out there too. One of you guys will have to drink this beer. I've gotta get back to my place before sundown. My old aunt promised to visit sometime in the next few days, and I've gotta be there for her whenever she shows up. I hope you'll both be okay. Nice to see you both when you're not being shot at. Rico, maybe in a day or two I'll drop by and make sure you're settled back in here...properly. Or I'll send Roxy."

"Now, Sally, that's...." Rico caught himself at the last minute. "That'd be just wonderful. I've been meaning to ask Roxy some serious questions. By all means send her over."

"Bye...bastard!" Grinning, Sally took her leave.

As she drove away, Mole could not help joining in. "Rico, did you ever get in Roxy's pants? I remember you saying they looked pretty tasty."

"*Pinche buey*, go screw yourself!"

At home again Sally lost no time in contacting Tom Dickannary. "Tom, the guy killed here in Idaho was Canunny. He was apparently ID'd by the sheriff through fingerprints and later confirmed to have been a CIA agent by another agent who was close to the loop. I just heard his name from the contact made by CIA out here. I also have word their agents are in Idaho looking at the murder scene and trying to scare everyone else off the case. Any connection yet with the other two dead guys?"

"Not yet. So Lando got outa Venezuela and ended up in backwoods Idaho. We don't know where he was in between. The guy must have been doing some sorta deal that involved the two Hollywood people, but that means they might've had some connection to Venezuela. This gets sticky, eh?"

"Yes it does. But it's not really our concern, is it?"

"Any missing agent from any DC agency gets NSA's attention, so yes, it's somewhat our concern, especially as it involves that rat's nest called Venezuela."

"Well, good luck. Keep me in the loop." Sally hung up the phone.

Sally peered at nothing out her window. She stood there a long time and finally said to herself, "What the dickens did dear Lando bring out of Venezuela?"

The next day Rico phoned Roxy Roades in DC. "Roxy, Rico Morgan. I have a request."

"Don't tell me you want to get me pregnant again?" She referred to her part in a previous adventure with Rico in old Mexico.

"I'd love to, but as someone said, that's not gonna happen."

"You never know, my friend. You never know."

"I'll take that as a good sign, Roxy, but this is a simpler thing. We've been told — my team and I — to stay out of an investigation into the deaths of a CIA guy and two TV-movie personalities. The guys who told us to keep out are CIA. Bledsome and Marsters. I wonder if you could keep your eyes open for anything around your DC offices that might relate to Molly Fender, Jimmy Fleetwing, and your man Canunny that could be grounds for us to keep our noses out of it. Is that asking too much? I know you're on the same team."

"I can do that, Rico, and if it looks like it'll help you...what are you tryin' to do anyway?"

"I guess find out who killed 'em. We have no real stake in the matter, not at this time. So we might do nothing."

"If I hear or see anything I can pass along I'll be sure to do so. How's Sally?"

"I'm not sure. She met us, Mole and I, when we got home and then she took off right away. Something about her aunt or cousin or grandmother coming to visit."

"Okay, take care of yourself. Bye."

No sooner did Rico hang up the landline when he got a call from Eileen Tudarite, the ex-stock trader in Rico's Boise Control who knew President Trump. "Rico, Yeats asked me to call you. I received information from a source in DC that there was a deal going down in Venezuela concerning another vast sum of money being transferred out. One of the people involved was the second-in-command to Maduro, Diosdado Cabello. The money involved was in the form of gold, apparently twenty tons of it. It was supposed to go to Turkey, along with a bunch of other Venezuelan assets, but its current location is unknown.

"Cabello's daughter, Daniela, was flown out about a week ago. That concerns us because there was apparently some contact between Daniela and the CIA agent called Canunny. He may have flown out with her. Canunny was arranging some extractions from VeeZee using CIA cargo aircraft, but from what we hear, he was supposed to stay in Venezuela. Since he disappeared, and has now been found dead, he's been replaced by another agent."

CARACAS CAPER

"Where's Daniela now?"

"We're not sure. The airplane on which she left the country landed first in Mexico City and then in Miami. If Canunny was on that flight he would most likely have got off in Miami. Daniela probably would have preferred Mexico, with her same language, and with Mexico still sympathetic to Maduro. So we guess she's there. The C-130 flew back to Venezuela directly from Miami."

"Eileen, do you have any sense of what might have caused Canunny to leave VeeZee? Any idea about the preservation of national finances, in any form?"

"All we know is Daniela is a lovely girl, single, uses social media — but her father uses it mostly for propaganda — and Canunny was youngish and fairly attractive. They appear to have been friends, but nothing is really certain about it. He might have left Caracas to be with her. As for the finances, generally Venezuela ships stuff to Turkey, and Erdogan has mentioned Turkey might give asylum to Maduro if he's kicked out. However, this lost gold did not go to Turkey."

Rico responded, "Okay, that's all logical. But if Lando stayed with her, like if he was her boyfriend, he'd have got off in Mexico. Or they both could have got off in Miami. We need to find her. Maybe Daniela knows why Lando zipped off to the Idaho back country. It would help to know where he went after he got off the C-130. Looks like he was moving fast, to get from either Mexico City or Miami into the back country here in Idaho in just a few days. Here's the thing: 'Canunny' per se didn't exist prior to about six years ago, so it's not his birth name. Can we find out who he was, perhaps by Yeats' prying?"

"I'll ask him. Anything else, Rico?"

"No. Thanks, Eileen, and best wishes to you."

CHAPTER 4
Boomer

It was mid-morning a few days after Rico and Mole got back from their aborted camping trip. Sally had yet to show up to 'settle' Rico properly. Roxy had not shown up either, which was not a surprise because she was in Washington, DC.

The two men sat at the breakfast table mulling over the events of the past few days. Rico made scrambled eggs with potato chunks that morning for the two of them and, the night before, made a big pot of his favorite coffee, organic dark Sumatra Mandheling.

Mole drained his coffee cup and said, "*Amigo*, it seems like a good idea for me to stick around here until you know a bit more about all this stuff, eh? I mean, I could go back to Las Cruces but I don't have anything to do there except wait for your phone call."

"Mole, you can stay in the guest bedroom as long as you want. It might save you a trip back and forth, if our guesses are right about the upcoming hiring of Rico Morgan and Company to look into...stuff that we don't know a friggin' thing about."

"*Sí, amigo*, we can sit on our thumbs here instead of camping out in the woods along the river for another coupla weeks like we planned. We can sit here waiting for the phone to ring when

CIA or NSA or XYZ hires us to find the missing whatzit that Canunny stole from Venezuela and gave to his supposed lover Daniela. And then we'll know, or can find out, what he buried along with all her kisses and his soul out here in Idaho just before he got his ass killed. And we can find out why he abandoned his job, left Venezuela and came here discretely to die. And they'll pay us for all this, y'see."

"Ah, that sums it up nicely, my friend. I was wondering what the heck was going on in this mess. Thanks for clearing it all up."

"And if they never call us I'll go home in a few months, and you can fly to DC and bone Roxy."

"C'mon. I'm with Sally. Would I ever do that?"

"Yes you would, given half a chance. Where's the coffee?"

A knock on the door shattered the pseudo-foggy haze of the two men. This was a rare occurrence for Rico, to have a knock on the door. Not very social by his own admission, Rico seldom to never had visitors come calling. Once in a while he was badgered by Jehovah's Witnesses, but that was not all bad because one of those religion-pushing visitors was a pilot, and he and Rico got along quite well. Sometimes the UPS man or FedEx guy would stop by. The FedEx guy was a gunny, and he and Rico always shot the breeze a while, but Rico didn't get many callers. So he acted appropriately to this knock.

With one hand on the hilt of his Colt CCO 45 auto, he peered out the kitchen window to see who it was. Then, a smile on his face, he went to the front door and opened it joyfully. Rico's near neighbor and good friend Joe Kelecztor was there with a big box in one hand and a sheaf of paper in the other.

"Hi, Joe, come on in. Coffee's on if you want some."

"Okay," said Joe, "I'll drink coffee and you can fill out all this paperwork. Not quite legal for me to bring this thing over to you, but I wanted to pick up that extra chain-saw blade and the two batteries you promised me last week but never delivered."

"Oops! Sorry about that. Whaja bring me, and what's all this paperwork?"

"It's for what's in the box. Just came in today. I haven't opened it yet, but it's from John Linebaugh."

"Aha!" Rico's eyes lit up. "It's the five hundred."

"The what?" asked Mole.

"John made me a 500 Linebaugh revolver. I told John to ship it to Joe so Joe could put it through his FFL. This hummer slings an ounce of lead at well over twelve hundred feet per second."

"Holy Moses!" said Mole. "Four hundred and forty grains? At over the speed of sound? No way!"

"Yes, way! Now we get to try it out, once Joe's happy with all the paperwork. Go ahead and open the box, Mole."

"What are you gonna do for ammo?" Mole asked as he dug into the padded carton and pulled out a Ruger box with the big revolver inside. He opened the box and withdrew a beautiful, blued, five-shot single-action revolver with fancy walnut stocks. The custom-made handgun was about the size of the old Colt Single-Action Army and weighed only a little more, but had a muzzle that was considerably more awesome, and had many times the power of the old frontier six-shooter.

"I got a few rounds from John a couple weeks ago. And I bought some from Tim Sundles down the road at Buffalo Bore, knowing this was coming."

Mole was awestruck. "Man! That Linebaugh guy does nice work," said Mole. "Look at all the flat areas on the frame. They're filed or stoned dead flat. The bluing is perfect! The lockup," he wiggled the cylinder, "is as tight as Roxy's ass."

"Hey!" Rico glanced up from filling out the federal forms for the receipt of the gun. "Watch it!"

"I did watch it. It looks tight!"

"What the heck are you guys talking about?" asked Joe, sitting at the table with a cup of coffee in one hand and a copy of the *American Rifleman* in the other.

"Nothing important," answered Rico. "Here's your paperwork. Many thanks. The chainsaw blade and the two batteries are there by the door. You wanna stick around and help us shoot this?"

"No, I've got stuff to do at home. Got my own guns to shoot if I get time." He grabbed his plunder and left.

"Let me run a patch through the bore and the cylinder before we try this hummer," said Rico. "I'll have to use shotgun patches. Don't have anything else big enough. I may have to use a 410 shotgun burr to get the patch to touch the rifling."

With the gun wiped clean of excess oil the two friends repaired to Rico's rifle range, which meant walking out the front door of Rico's house. They turned left and walked past the house to his hundred-yard rifle-target butt, which Rico made years before from a huge dead and downed cottonwood cut and stacked to form a positive bullet stop.

Rico attached a fifty-yard pistol target to the wood target holder. He then stepped back twenty yards, put one round into the 500 Linebaugh, made sure his ear and eye protectors were on good and tight, took a modified Weaver stance, aimed at the paper target on the backstop and gently pressed the trigger. The mighty gun roared, shoved Rico's hands skyward, and gave two outstanding results: a large hole near the center of the paper target, and a huge grin on Rico's face.

"Thank you, John Linebaugh!" Rico was ecstatic. "This sixgun...er, five-gun, has enough power to drop an elephant but doesn't kill the shooter if he's aware of what he's doing. But I sure wouldn't want to run fifty or even ten rounds through this in a hurry. My hand would be numb for days. Your turn, Mole. Be sure to not lock your elbow."

Modesto loaded the gun, again with only one round, and using only one hand, arm extended straight from the shoulder, elbow slightly bent, fired the powerful revolver. His hand ended up pointed at the sky behind his head. "Zowie!" he yelled. "That is one incredible handgun, my friend. My hat's off to Mr. Linebaugh. He combined the Bisley grip with the fine mechanics of the Ruger and his own custom work, and ended up with a controllable, handy, extremely powerful revolver. I'm impressed! My hand is impressed too, still tingling, but I could shoot it again if I had to."

The two men fired a few more rounds, and then went back to Rico's house. Rico set about cleaning the gun with Mole watching.

Mole picked up the custom five-shot cylinder and gave it a close examination while Rico worked on cleaning the barrel. "That's really nice workmanship, good clean machining. But Rico, why'd you buy this theeng? I know you don't hunt any more."

"Just to add it to the collection, my friend. Maybe carry it a time or two. I've known John Linebaugh a long time and wanted to have one of his fine creations in my vault. Ya know, he's among the rarest of the gun makers, because he has his name on a bona-fide SAAMI cartridge before he's dead and buried."

"This one?"

"No, the 475 Linebaugh, which is essentially the same, maybe even a bit more powerful, but doesn't fling the heaviest bullets."

"That's impressive. I suppose you could stop a Mack truck with that thing if you had to."

"Seriously, they've killed elephant with these. I hope I never have to try to stop a truck, or an elephant for that matter. I also know I'll have to avoid shooting it for few days if I'm gonna play any musical instrument. John told me he plays guitar now and keeps strictly away from these, and especially his bigger boomers."

"Bigger?! Bigger than this?"

"Yeah, the so-called 475 and 500 Linebaugh Longs put this one to shame. And I suspect they'd destroy your hands in a trice if you shot 'em much."

"What's a trice?"

"Faster than a bice."

"I see."

With the gun cleaned and stored in Rico's vault the two men sat and discussed what they'd avoided as long as they could.

Rico started it. "Mole, the guy who stole the canoe has to be the one who killed the three folks out there. Unless...."

"Unless there was more than one killer who snuck through the woods past us to the canoe. But then...."

"The canoe could have been stolen by someone else and the killer or killers are still out in the woods, running in the other direction. What are the chances of that?"

"Possible, but unlikely."

"We can't eliminate that possibility."

"¡No, Señor! We're pretty sure the killer stole something, but maybe he just whacked the three victims for some other reason.

If it was just a question of stealing some odd, valuable item there'd be no great reason to kill them...."

"So they must have known something, or saw something fatal to them. What if the CIA guy, Lando, hijacked them to come along, maybe as protection?"

Mole thought about that for a moment, stopping the rapid-fire, back-and-forth discussion. "Could Molly Fender have been doing a story that connects them all?"

"Excellent idea. Let's find out what she was working on. I can get Boise Control to look into it with a phone call." Rico made a quick phone call and went back to contemplation of the lunch Mole had set out for them on the kitchen table. It consisted of cheese, good bread, apples, a pile of raisins, an insulated pitcher of hot coffee, and a few donuts. "Mole, how'd you like a job as full-time *criada*?"

"I ain't yore maid, *hijo*. You cain't afford me nohow, anyway."

An hour later Yeats at Boise Control called back and told them the story. "Rico, Miss Fender was indeedy doing a story of some importance to Canadians. A few days before she was killed she flew to the Dominion Diamond Mines headquarters, up in Calgary, along with Mr. Fleetwing the ex-magician, and a camera crew to take a look at, and do a story on the huge yellow diamond found at the Diavik diamond mine. Diavik is in the Northwest Territories and is partially owned by Dominion. This is the largest diamond ever mined on this continent. It was discovered late last year and made worldwide news. The stone is about the size of a hen's egg."

"Aha! Now we're getting somewhere. Diamonds!"

Mole's face lit up when Rico said that word.

"Where is the diamond now? Still in Calgary?" Rico wiped his hand over his eyes, as though waking from a dream.

"Presumably, but we don't know for sure."

"Calgary's almost due north of Idaho, and only about five hundred air miles from the death site. Yeats, I suspect we're getting somewhere. *Bravo, bravissimo!*"

Mole stared out the big window overlooking the stream that ran through Rico's property. "The killer could have had a radio, which is likely, and told the pickup pilot to meet him somewhere else, maybe in a few days. We need to find that pickup chopper and ask him. I have its N number."

"Good idea. Also, the canoe might have some fingerprints on it that are not ours, nor Paul's, nor those of the guy who found it." Rico rubbed his neck. "We better ask the sheriff if he looked."

"No, Rico, we can't. Don'tcha remember those CIA guys told us to not get involved?"

"Balls and buttfucker!"

"Thinking about Roxy again?"

"No, asshole, those two goons at the sheriff's office."

"I thought they were Rectum and Anus."

"Close enough! Please leave Roxy's tasty trousers outa this."

"Now, how would you *know* they're tasty? Unless...."

Rico threw a donut at Mole.

CHAPTER 5
Rethinking

The next day Rico phoned Sheriff Lutz at North Bedford and put the question of fingerprints on the canoe to him.

"Morgan, I won't admit it, but despite the two goons who said keep out of it, I did look for prints on the canoe. I found nothing new, though. "

"Thanks, sheriff. We'll keep in touch with you."

"Rico, check this out!" Mole was on Rico's computer looking at a website devoted to a helicopter company out of Lewiston, Idaho, which was within easy range of the location of the murders. "The bird we saw there is owned by this company. What say we call 'em, or go up there and talk with the pilot, to see if he can tell us who he took out to the wilds along with that TV woman and the actor."

"Be easier to phone 'em, see what they say. I'd suspect they'll recall the famous TV woman, and maybe the actor."

Mole called the listed number and after a suitable delay got through to Moses Wright, the flight director of the company. "Mr. Wright, this is Michael Dorstreet with GSI investigations out of Lewiston." Mole lied convincingly. "I wonder if you can tell us the name of the pilot who took Molly Fender, Jimmy

Fleetwing, and two other guys on that flight into the Idaho back country a short time ago." Mole gave the exact date.

"Yeah, sure, that was Ralph Tracer. But there were only three passengers in the bird. Someone else asked me yesterday, how I know. I looked it up on the manifest. Is anything wrong? Anything new on this?"

"No, not that we know of. We know your pilot came back to the drop-off area but didn't land to pick anyone up. We assume you are aware of that."

"Yes, sir. When I saw the empty chopper land I asked him where the pick-ups were, and he told the simple truth. He could see the dead people on the ground, chose to not land, and flew out of there to report it to the sheriff's office. But the sheriff already knew."

"Thank you, sir. We may call you again."

"*Riicoo!!*" Mole shouted as soon as the land-line phone hit the cradle.

"What?"

"There were only three people flown out to the killing site, not four like we guessed."

"The hell you say!"

"Yeh. Let's retheenk this whole friggin' affair, *amigo*. With only three in the chopper the killer had to be there already. Someone else brought him in and would be the one to pick him up. He didn't *expect* to get picked up by the chopper, the one we saw. That chopper came to get the three, circled the field, saw 'em dead and bleedin' on the ground, flew back home and actually reported the crime, which I just found out. But by the time the pilot called it in, we'd already told Paul to bring the sheriff."

"Okay. Then the killer had to have his own way to get out. He'd radio for a pickup when needed. When he — or she, or they — heard us, they chose to leave by canoe, so they didn't need to call for pickup, so we saw only the one innocent chopper. But if the killer had been there already, waiting...."

"There'd probably be some signs of his camping out. Now, the CIA would have found that, and said something. Unless...."

"Unless the killer was CIA. Then they wouldn't want us looking into it, nor the sheriff either. But if that's the case, and as we know, Lando was CIA, why'd Lando get killed? Was he just a patsy?"

"Man! Rico, this sucks big time."

Rico wanted a Scotch but held off. He grabbed a cigar, offered one to Mole, and they headed out the door to smoke in the clear sunny yard. They walked along the back trail leading from Rico's house past the target butt upstream, away from the highway. In a peaceful spot under a huge ponderosa, high above the stream flowing through Rico's property, the men sat on the ground and lit their stogies. Rico knew that serious contemplation called for serious cigars, and these were Arturo Fuente Hemingway Signatures.

Rico brought the problem up again. "Okay. Why'd the three fly there? Where'd they come from and what could they be doing in such a remote spot as that?"

"Clearly they flew out of Lewiston, but we can't trace 'em before that."

"Yes we can!," said Rico. "Yeats says they did an interview in Calgary, just north of there, with the diamond people. Is there a chance they stole some diamonds?"

"Mebbe." Mole blew smoke rings into the clear mountain air. "We know Canunny was in Venezuela, then he next appears to us in Lewiston in the company of two TV people who had just come from Calgary, only for all three to get killed in the back country. Most likely they were going to meet the guy or guys who were already deep in the woods there, presumably camped out. Maybe get a payoff for the diamonds they stole? Maybe transfer stuff they didn't want seen, like drugs? *Pues, hombre, yo no sé.*"

"Hold on a minute. Let's say you and I were gonna meet someone and were flown in by helicopter. Wouldn't we just tell the pilot to wait? Clearly they sent him away with a message to come back later in the day." Rico sucked earnestly on his stogie.

"Yeh, Rico, good point. They wanted him gone. Must have been something going on that the trio and whoever else was there didn't want anyone to witness. Maybe the fourth guy was someone special. I doubt this deal was drugs, because the chopper pilot would have seen a package the trio were carrying, or something else that could be full of drugs. Maybe a knapsack."

Rico sat back against the big tree. "Knapsack or even a backpack is a possibility. Canunny was dressed like he could stay in the woods a while, so he might have had a pack, but not Molly nor Jimmy, not in their fancy clothes."

Mole blew more smoke rings. "It could have been something small and valuable other than diamonds. Maybe some electronic stuff, or some sort of high-tech device they wanted to test but didn't want seen."

"Hmm. If it was a high-tech laser or other clever mil-spec-type device, that's another good reason to send the chopper away." Rico tried blowing smoke rings and choked on the smoke. "Here's another dire possibility," he coughed out. "What if Lando was going to kill them and either leave with the other guy or stay there camped a while? That'd be a good reason to send the chopper away."

"Yeah, but they ordered the chopper back, so that's not right. They wouldn't want it to come back for dead bodies. It looks like they were planning on the two TV people gettin' outa there via chopper and Lando going on with the guy who was already there, based on their clothes, if nothing else."

Rico blew through his cigar before he let it go out, so the nasty smoke and foulness would not be there when he relit it later. "If that's the case, then that means the guy who was there double-crossed Lando. Maybe the plan was to kill all three right from the start, and take whatever they brought to the meeting. But if the killer was supposed to be picked up by his own team, does that mean he double-crossed them too?"

"Maybe." Mole contemplated that a while. "If he had a radio, which is almost certain, he could have told his team he had a different way to get out of the woods, by stealing our canoe. That means they wouldn't need to send a pick-up bird. So, whatever the trio brought there, say diamonds because that seems most likely, was taken by the killer who then saw our canoe as a chance to get out without his team picking him up. If he hadn't told his team about the canoe they'd have sent a chopper to pick him up. We saw only the one, the innocent chopper. So he must've told them. What we don't know is if the triple murder was part of the original plan all along. I suspect it was not."

Rico said, "If the killer was supposed to take Lando with him and leave the TV guys, but shot Lando and the others instead, that gives us a rogue team member. A rogue CIA man on the run with a bag of diamonds."

"Nuts!" said Mole. "How'd they get a bag of diamonds out of the diamond company in the first place? One would think they have security there."

"I dunno. Magic?" Rico pocketed his dead cigar stub.

And on that note the two friends abandoned the discussion and returned to the house for dinner.

42

That evening another phone call broke the peace of Rico's house. It was Yeats, calling on behalf of Boise Control. "Mr. Morgan, sir, we have some information about the Canadians. One of us — I won't say who — managed to find out that the birth name of the so-called Lando Canunny was William Fehnder. Mr. Fehnder was in fact...wait for it, please...also a Canadian. He became a U.S. citizen about a decade ago. Prior to that he lived in a small town...."

Rico interrupted him. "About fifty miles out of Ottawa, called Perth. Did you say William Fender?"

"No, Fehnder, with an aitch."

A long pause, and then Rico said, "Yeats, for the love of God find out if Molly Fender used to have an aitch in her name."

An hour later Yeats called back. "Mr. Morgan, I have two pieces of information for you, kind sir. Yes, indeedy, Molly Fender used to have an aitch in her name. Birth records in Perth, Ontario, Canada, gave us that information and also that she has a younger brother, first name William."

"Hmm. Okay, so Molly and Lando are brother and sister. Were. So he probably wasn't about to kill his sister and the other guy."

"Yes, the former magician."

"The what?"

"I mentioned to you that Mr. Fleetwing, back in 2009 and 2010, was a sleight-of-hand-magic man. He was quite good at it from what we see here. We found a YouTube video of him making things disappear or change into other items. It is most fascinating, yes indeedy."

"Yeats, that gives me an idea. Anything else?"

"Yes indeedy. Our man Byron Summers has found something that might be of interest to you. He was given high-resolution images of the area where the three people were killed, based on the GPS information derived from your satellite-message machine. Please don't ask how he got them. Mr. Summers scanned them carefully and he saw something the federal agents did not discover, or perhaps intentionally overlooked."

"What's it look like?"

"Mr. Summers says there appears to be a crude lean-to or perhaps a small tent and the remnants of a campfire located on the very top of the crag next to the clear area where the murders took place. It appears as though someone had been camped out there for some time."

"And our fed friends didn't find this? I thought they went over that area extremely carefully. Or did they just fail to mention it?"

"The hideout lean-to was well camouflaged, but the rain and wind that came through that area last week moved some of the brush, and that is why Mr. Summers was able to see the lean-to."

"Damn. We might have to put dear old Byron on the payroll. Okay, Yeats. Thank you kindly for the information. Anyone hire us yet?"

"No indeedy."

"Later, my friend." Rico put down the phone and walked to the window and looked at the sun setting over the western mountains. He relayed the gist of the message from Yeats to Modesto.

"Mole, is there any reason to go have a look at that camp in the clearing? What're the chances the CIA didn't already go over it completely, and white-wash whatever was there?"

"Negative, *amigo*, they couldn't have. Yeats said Byron Summers found the image only yesterday, long after the CIA was in there on the ground. The goons were in there right after we got outa there. They probably thought our camp, where we spent the night waiting for the chopper, was the one used by their man. So this campsite on top of the crag was *not* looked at by them, or it would'a been covered up or destroyed by them. If they'd done that, your man Byron wouldn't have seen anything. But he *did*."

"Crap, Mole, you're right. I guess we should go have a look at it. There might be something there that tells us a bit more about this mess.

CHAPTER 6
Backtracking

Two weeks before the three people were killed in the Idaho back country, Diosdado Cabello's aide Raúl Sanchez met with Lando Canunny in a small office in Caracas, Venezuela. Sanchez was a small, natty man with a clipped moustache, and hair going gray all over. He was fifty-seven years old. He wore a nearly new, light-gray suit with red tie over his slightly pear-shaped body. His piercing black eyes tried to bore a hole in the fit man of twenty-seven years standing in front of his desk.

"*Señor* Canunny, I can now assure you *Señor* Cabello will be happy to alter the shipment to arrive in Ottawa, not Ankara, if you can indeed deliver the item offered. As you know, both Daniela and her father *Señor* Cabello are fond of such nice things as you have offered. I wonder how you are going to obtain it, as it must surely be heavily guarded."

"I have a plan. I am quite sure I can lay hands on the item in the next week or so. I can then deliver it to you here, or wherever you choose to accept delivery."

"Here in Caracas would be fine."

"Then I will be back shortly. I'm going to leave on the next cargo plane with Daniela and some of her things. In light of the increasing acceptance of Juan Guaidó throughout the world and the resultant possibility — nearly a guarantee — of hostilities here, she has decided to emigrate to Mexico until things are more settled here in Venezuela."

"¡*Bueno!* Then we will be in communication in the near future, my friend."

A little over a week later Lando Canunny flew to Mexico City in the company of Daniela Cabello and a half-dozen large trunks of her finery. They got off at the terminal in Mexico City where Dani took a taxi to the estate of a wealthy friend of Maduro's, along with her many trunks of swag. Lando Canunny checked into a handy hotel for the night, and made a few phone calls.

Early the next day Lando took a flight from the Mexican capitol that landed him first in Denver. As Lando sat in the departure lobby reading a magazine and waiting for the next leg of his flight, a youngish man in a cheap brown suit and carrying a briefcase sat down next to him. Brown-suit put the briefcase on his lap. Lando glanced at him and said nothing. After a few minutes the young-looking man asked Lando, "How's the view in Cuba?"

Lando responded, "It's full of tits."

The cheap-suit man again asked, "How does one deal with that?"

Lando replied, "I have to keep my trousers on."

"What color are your trousers?"

"Peachy fuckin' purple."

The youngish man in the cheap brown suit opened the briefcase, took out a small wooden box, closed the briefcase, and handed the box to Lando Canunny. Brown-suit stood up and walked away.

Lando put the box in his pocket and went back to his magazine.

A few hours later, with suitable flight links, Lando arrived in Calgary, Alberta, Canada. That night he dined with his sister, Molly Fehnder, aka Molly Fender the TV personality.

"Sis, I've got the egg that my boys made for me. I won't show it because someone might see, but it's an exact copy, as good as could be done." The two of them sat, waiting for a third to join them, before ordering.

Molly replied, "That's great, Bill." She smiled at her younger brother 'Lando,' whose birth name was William Fehnder.

"Where's Jimmy, eh?" Lando referred to James Flitzenwanger, whom the world knew as Jimmy Fleetwing, the actor from *Busting Ground*.

"He should be here already. He said fifteen minutes and it's been twenty-five. Might've got stuck in traffic."

"Here he is!" Lando stood up and shook hands with the tall, handsome, movie-and-TV star who strode manfully up to their table.

Just before Jimmy Fleetwing sat down he waved his hand dramatically in the air and a white rose appeared in it, which he presented to Molly Fender.

"Up to your old sleight-of-hand tricks, I see," said Molly with the trace of a blush on her pretty face.

"Yep! Gotta keep my hand in if this deal is going to work like we hope it is." He took his seat, and when the waiter came and poured the wine, they all ordered simple and relatively fast meals. Jimmy raised his wine glass to the other two. "May this deal go perfectly, my friends." They touched glasses in a toast.

"When is your interview with the company, eh?" Lando asked his sister.

"This Thursday."

Jimmy raised his glass again, looked through the red liquid at the light behind it, and said, "Today's Tuesday, so that gives us all tomorrow to practice."

The three drank, ate, talked, and departed with the agreement to meet the following day to 'rehearse,' as Jimmy put it, in Molly's hotel room.

Thursday of that week the three met outside the headquarters of Dominion Diamond Mines. "Here we go," said Molly. "Do you have it?" she asked Jimmy.

"It's in my coat pocket where I can get it instantly, but it'll never show," he replied.

Molly's photo crew for the TV show *Fun For Your Life* were there with her, all ready to go inside and film her interview with the head of Diavik Diamond Mine, where the largest diamond ever found in North America was discovered in late 2018.

The rough uncut stone weighs 552 carats, has a strong yellowish color, and is about the size of a hen's egg. In its uncut state it has a rugged exterior, bearing the abrading marks of the screening process. Following the announcement of the discovery dozens of detailed photos of the stone appeared on several media websites. The photos showed the rugged, scarred exterior in fine detail and illustrated nicely its pale yellow hue. The copy accompanying the photos gave its exact dimensions.

Molly, her brother Bill, her friend Jimmy, and the TV filming and recording crew were shown into a room with a guard at the entry door. Inside, they passed into yet another room, this one relatively small. Again an armed guard stood by the door, and inside the room were three more armed guards. In the center of the room was a pedestal with a Plexiglas cover, under which resided the huge rough diamond.

After the TV crew and Molly and her people were in the room, two well-dressed men came in. The first one spoke. "Hi, Molly. I recognize you from your TV show. I'm David Blunt, associate head of Dominion Diamond Mines and CEO of Diavik Mine. This is my associate Henry Wanker from Rio Tinto, based in London." Molly shook hands with both.

"Miss Fender, we're glad you're here." Henry Wanker spoke with a London accent. "We understand you want to do a show-and-tell for your TV audience and we're glad to be of assistance. Where do we start?"

Molly launched into her interview with the cameras rolling. All went well for nearly an hour, with the Britisher and the Canadian CEO fielding all her questions and giving quite a bit of the history of diamond mining in Canada. Molly and her crew were astonished to find out that Canada was third of the world's nations in the production of diamonds, producing nearly fourteen million carats in 2017. The top two nations in the world in diamond production were Botswana in number two spot and, a big surprise again to the visitors, Russia at the top of the heap with nearly twenty-three million carats of diamond production in 2017. The numbers for 2018 were not yet available, they were told, but it looked like Russia would do even better, and Canada might even surpass Botswana for second place.

Near the end of her interview Molly Fender asked the directors a favor. "Gentlemen, as you know I've brought Jimmy Fleetwing, the actor, with me, and we'd like to pose a shot that will be the lead-in to my interview. I'd like Mr. Fleetwing to hold the stone in one hand, and he'll raise his other hand as though he were holding a pistol, so the image will be sort of

James Bond-like. We'll add the pistol in post-production, and we believe it'll make an eye-catching image for the viewing audience. Is that possible? Can we have Mr. Fleetwing briefly hold the stone?"

"Yes, of course." David Blunt spoke. "Our security here is overt, but it's not really necessary. Most of it was done for your interview, so it would look to your audience like we were being extremely careful about the stone. Which, of course, we are."

Mr. Henry Wanker from London explained. "The stone is unique and already well known. Even if it were the object of mad desire of a James Bond, or actually in his possession, it could not fail to be recognized throughout the world. By all means pose your photo shoot. We look forward to viewing it."

David Blunt got a key and after several deft twists in various semi-concealed locations, lifted off the Plexiglas cover, picked up the huge diamond and handed it to Jimmy Fleetwing.

The TV crew posed Jimmy in several spy-like video scenes and then Jimmy handed the diamond back to Mr. Blunt. Mr. Blunt carefully wiped it and put it back under its protective cover.

The interview was over, and Molly Fender and her crew filed out of the offices of the diamond company.

CHAPTER 7
Rendezvous

"So, where the hell are we going?" Jimmy Fleetwing asked Lando Canunny as they drove south toward Lewiston, Idaho, the day after the interview with the CEO of the diamond mine.

"We're going to Lewiston, and from there we're flying to a remote spot in western Idaho so my people — CIA — can land there without calling attention to themselves in one of their big black military choppers. They'll take me and the stone from there to Boise and then we'll be flown directly to Venezuela. You guys come along so we don't lose track of the stone or each other until we get paid, eh?"

"A quarter mil?" Jimmy asked.

"No, a third. A mil split three ways. My sis will take care of my pile and hers, and I'll depart with the military chopper, back to Venezuela. I was the guy who made the deal with Cabello's man, so they expect me back there."

"So why are you dressed like a bum?" Molly Fender asked her brother.

"I may need to camp out in the woods, eh? I was told the guy waiting for us there has been there a few days, and it might take a while for the coordination of the pickup chopper. The guy in the woods has our money, so that'll be all right.

"Lando?" Molly spoke. Over the past days she'd got used to calling her brother by his 'new' name.

"What?"

"Once the diamond company figures out the stone is phony won't they suspect my crew and us, for the theft?"

"Sure, but we're taking a chance they won't discover it for a long time. Maybe weeks, eh. They're planning the cutting operation now, and that'll take a lot of time on the part of the cutters. They won't need to look at the stone again, eh. They've got videos and photos of it from every angle to help them plan how best to cut it. Once it's found out to be phony it'll be long gone. They can suspect you and your crew but they told us security wasn't a big problem. If the stone ever turns up again they'll be the bona-fide owners and will get it back...somehow, eh?"

"That sounds over-simplified, Lando."

"I agree." Jimmy spoke up from the back seat. "Won't they come after us big time?"

"Not until they discover it's a fake."

"What if it ain't a fake?" Jimmy asked.

"Whadda ya mean?"

"What if I told you the stone in your pocket is still the fake one?"

"What the heck are you talking about, James?" Lando lifted his foot from the accelerator and the rental car began to slow down on the nearly empty highway.

"Let's say I bobbled the switcheroo and was unable to do the job?"

"Jesus Christ! Did you?"

"I might've."

Lando pulled the car over to the side of the road and shut off the engine. He took the stone out of his pocket, unwrapped it from the soft cloth it was in, and stared at it. "Damn! I can't tell if it's real or fake."

"Exactly!" Jimmy gave a wry smile. "So no one else can, either. But it's the real thing. My quick switch didn't get noticed by anyone there. I've still got the 'ol touch! Thing is, once you pass it along to Cabello or his daughter, how'll they know it's real or not?"

"They might have it inspected as soon as it hits their hands. I sure would if my ass depended on it, eh?"

"Wait," said Molly. "They're not gonna cut it, at least not right away. All they want is possession of the stone to make them do whatever it is you want them to do. Isn't that the setup?"

"Yeah."

Jimmy interrupted. "How far along the path will the stone go before someone tries to inspect it to see if it's real or not?"

"Probably not until long after it gets to Cabello...and he plans to give it to his daughter," replied Lando.

"Well, there ya are! It might as well be fake, even though it's real."

Lando thought about this for a minute or two. Finally he started the car going again. He remarked, "Real or fake, it don't affect us in any way. But you're sure this is the real one, eh?"

"Absolutely," replied Jimmy Fleetwing.

The three continued south towards Lewiston, Idaho.

"Okay, Mr. Pilot, we'd like you to take us to this location." Lando handed him a set of coordinates.

"Muh name's Ralph," said Ralph Tracer, one of the handful of helicopter pilots working for Highman Choppers out of Lewiston. "What is this place? Looks like it's deep in the back country right smack between no and where. The river is pretty close to it, very near it, I see."

"There's a clearing there, I guarantee you. Check your satellite image and you'll see it."

"By gum, there it is," spoke Ralph, peering at a computer screen. "Okay, what's the deal? You wanna git dropped off thar?"

"Yes, all three of us. I'm going to stay there for a few days and then hike out with my buddy, who's already there. But now, listen, you'll have to leave all three of us for most of the day and then come back just before dark to pick up my sister and our friend. They're not staying, but we need to be alone for a while, eh?"

"Okay." Ralph Tracer was not one to ask questions about why his passengers might want to do something. That was their business. His business was flying, and complying with any odd requests along the way. "Thet's cheaper'n havin' me set on the ground all day waitin' for y'all." Ralph spat a jet of tobacco juice into the bushes at the edge of the airport where they were standing. "D'ya have any camping gear?"

"No, my friend came down there by river and has everything I need. Sleeping bag, tent, food, the works, eh? He radioed me once he got settled."

"No gear o' yer own? Seems a mite strange."

"Yeh, but I was up in Canada. Couldn't get away any sooner so we had to do it this way, with my buddy bringing my gear along. I did a job there with my sister here, whom you may recognize. She's Molly Fender. Has a TV show, eh?"

"Cain't say I do," said Ralph. "Sorry, ma'am. I don't watch much TV. How soon ya wanna go?"

"We can head out right now if your bird's ready to fly."

"'Tis. Let's git loaded...er, load the helicopter, I mean."

Ralph flew the three people on a smooth and fast flight in his Jet Ranger to the cleared area near the river, set them down gently, and flew away.

"Where's the guy we're supposed to meet?" asked Jimmy.

"He's camped out here somewhere. I guess if he's not we'll just wait 'til the bird comes back near sundown and we'll have had a fine day in the woods." Lando licked his lip. He didn't like it that the person who was supposed to be there had yet to show. The three had been there close to half an hour.

"He should've heard the helicopter," said Lando's sister Molly.

"You'd think so," replied Lando. "Oh! There he is!" He pointed to the side of the huge crag, where a man had just stepped out of the woods and was walking toward them. The three went to greet him. He was wearing green camo military garb and combat boots. He had a pistol in what appeared to be a regulation holster at his side.

Lando knew the man but didn't want his sister nor Jimmy to know that.

"Hi," said Lando. You must be the guy we're waiting to see."

"Yes, replied the man. I presume you're Lando Canunny and these are Molly Fender and Jimmy Fleetwing?"

All three agreed and shook hands with the stranger. "What's your name?" asked Molly.

"My name is unimportant. I'd give you a fake one anyway in light of what's going on here."

"I understand," she replied.

Jimmy asked, "Do you have something for us? Because we have something for you."

"Yes. I presume you have a yellow rock for me?"

"And you have a large box of bills for us?" Lando asked.

"Let me see the stone and I'll take you to the box of bills, which is over at the edge of the woods."

Lando took out the carefully wrapped rock and held it out for the 'stranger' to see. The stranger didn't try to take it.

"Good!" he said. "Let's walk toward the south end of the clearing. That's where the box with the, er, bills is. Pretty big box, too."

Lando said, "I'm supposed to be going with you outa here, but our delivery chopper will come back near sundown to take these two home. Do you have a way to call for pick up for us here?"

"Yep. I've got a radio. I been here three days. Didn't know when you'd show up. Got a campsite up on the hill, out of the way. Be nice to get out and get some decent food."

The four people approached the south end of the clearing. No box was in sight.

"Where's this big box?" Jimmy asked.

"Change of plans, friends," said the stranger. He had been trailing behind the trio. They turned to face him and saw he had his handgun out and pointed at them.

Molly gave a loud shriek. She realized the situation instantly. If she and Jimmy were allowed to live and return to her TV show the heat would be on them for the theft of the diamond. If she and Jimmy suddenly disappeared, the theft would just be a larger mystery. They could never be questioned. "No! **NO!**" she cried.

She screamed again just as the man fired his weapon. Three fast shots and it was over.

The stranger searched the pockets of Lando and found the huge yellow uncut diamond. He pocketed it and walked back towards his little camp up on the crag, but when he was about to climb up to it he heard sounds breaking the complete stillness of the wild Idaho back country. The sounds came from the direction of the river. He heard the grating noise a canoe makes when it's beached on the edge of the river.

The faint light of an idea glowed suddenly in his head. During the three days he was camped there the killer had found an old game trail that led from the top of the crag where he was camped down to the river by a round-about route. Could he? Yes, he could, he told himself. At least he could try.

He climbed the crag and gathered one or two important items of his gear from his well-concealed camp, leaving most of it there. Then, quickly and quietly, he took the animal's way down from his perch. The game trail took him first north, away from the clearing, and then west towards the river, circling the clear area in the rugged mountain terrain. He was thus completely out of sight of anyone who might be coming toward the clearing from the river.

At the edge of the river, just north of where the canoe was beached and tethered, the killer climbed silently down the rocks on the old game trail. He undid the craft's painter, eased the canoe gently into the stream, got in and headed downstream to the south. He radioed his helicopter crew not to bother with an extraction. He was on his way home.

———————

CHAPTER 8
Camping

"**S**ally, you might be aware of the proposed concerts and musical gatherings at the border between Venezuela and Colombia. How'd you feel about participating? There's an orchestra heading there to play some Bach and other classics for the people, to encourage good feelings and possibly help to get more supplies and food delivered into the country. They could use a good fiddler." Tom Dickannary in Washington, DC, spoke to Sally Foarth on the phone at her Idaho home.

"Gee, Tom, what is it you want me to try to find out down there?" Sally had her violin bow dangling from her finger. The Guarneri was on a softly padded table next to her music stand, which held Paganini's Sonate I, Op. 2 for violin and guitar, the adagio portion. The phone had interrupted one of Sally's daily practice sessions, the necessary bane of the concert solo violinist. Sally knew the request for her to visit the border of the troubled country meant that someone in DC wanted her to go to work as the part-time NSA agent she was, and dig something out of someone down there.

"We know it's a long shot, and you may not even be able to get into the country, but we're looking for anything, anything at all, that might help us find twenty tons of gold that's disappeared. It's not our gold but we want to know if it's still in the country, or if they managed to ship it out. If so, where'd it go? If you can get into Venezuela as a first-class musician the chances of your meeting with top government personnel there would be high, and a few discrete questions might get you the information we seek."

"A few discrete questions to the wrong guys might get me a jail sentence from those clowns. I'll have to think it over, Tom, and get back to you. I'm all for going, but I can't see that it'll do anyone any good if I can't get into VeeZee."

"Thanks, Sally. All best." Tom broke the connection.

Sally's phone rang again that afternoon. It was Rico. "Hi, darlin', howd'ja like to go camping?"

"Can I bring my fiddle? I just got a request to do a concert."

"Yeah, but you might want to bring your cheapest one. Not the Guarneri, nor even the Keith Hill. One of those German Strad copies you have would sound plenty good out in the woods, especially one of those your neighbor took apart and scraped into sounding somewhat better."

"Where are we going?"

"Back to the site where the three people were killed. Unless you'd rather not."

"Why?"

"Why what?"

"Why go? I mean, you were just there."

"One of my men found a campsite there no one has looked at. It might lead to some information in this weary case we're pokin' at."

Sally thought about that a few seconds. "Aren't you supposed to stay away from it? I mean, is anyone paying you anything for poking around?"

"Not yet, but there's always a chance, especially if we have some information no one else has, and this might be one way to get it."

"When are we going?"

"Tomorrow, if you can get away. Mole sez he might sit this one out, to give us some time alone."

"Hell, he can come. Can he bring a date? And how long are we staying?'

"No, no date. Doesn't know anyone up here. We'll be out just one night, but it'll take another half-day to go there and a half to drive back. So figure two days total. Paul will drop us off and pick us up the next day. Are you sure about Mole coming along? He might not like the sound of us ruttin' like badgers in the night. Might go off and nab him some poor wild critter and make his own ruttin' noises, just to get even."

"What makes you so sure we'll be doing any 'ruttin'?"

"One can only hope."

"What time?"

"The train pulls out at eight ayem. And I've got a sleeping bag for you."

"Count me in."

The next morning the 'train,' which was Rico's immaculate old dark-green Dodge Stealth R/T Twin Turbo, took Rico, Sally and Mole to North Bedford, where Paul Gobbarander flew them, three sleeping bags, some easily carried food, water, a few other supplies, plus the makings of a simple lean-to back to the death scene. "I'll be back around four tomorrow afternoon, Rico. You guys have a good time."

"Thanks, Paul. Will do."

"Where were the victims, Rico? I don't want to go near that spot." Sally shuddered.

"Over there to the south about fifty yards. We'll go into the woods here to the east, and set up a camp to the side of this big crag. The spot we've got to inspect is up at its top." The crag towered over the clearing, rising into the sky a hundred and fifty feet above where they stood. The back of the crag blended into the steep mountainside behind it. All of it was thick with lodgepole pine and significant underbrush.

The group found a suitable spot at the edge of the woods, set up the lean-to and cleared the ground for a fire. It was late afternoon by the time everything was done and camp was essentially all set up.

"Rico, do we want to go up top tonight?" Mole looked toward the setting sun. "We don't have a lot of light left."

"What say we relax for the night, enjoy ourselves a little, and do our examination in the morning?"

"Sounds like a good idea," Mole said.

"There's no hurry, is there?" Sally asked. "I mean, the camp up there's been sitting all by itself for a while now, hasn't it?"

Rico nodded. "That's right. It's not going anywhere, and so far as we know we're the only ones who know there's anything up there."

"So," said Sally, "let's get some dinner going, and then maybe have a look around here at ground level. Except for the south side, where you found the bodies." Sally broke out the bag with the utensils and the easily portable food, and Rico and Mole gathered wood for the cooking fire.

The night came gently and easily as they cooked, made the camp more comfortable, and set out their pads and sleeping bags under the lean-to. By the time it was full dark the trio had eaten and were sharing stories of old times, reviving memories of old camping trips, and enjoying some good bottled beer.

Later, when it was time to turn in, Mole said, "Guys, I'll be back in about half an hour, maybe longer. Give you some time to yourselves." Without another word he disappeared into the darkness.

"What's that all about?" asked Sally.

"I have no idea." Rico started to get into his sleeping bag.

"Er, Rico, do we have time, er, to *do* anything? Isn't that why Mole disappeared?"

"No, I think we've gotta keep some sort of lookout, maintain our decency, and take care to not get surprised by any of the critters around here."

Sally gave a shrug to the night air, convinced she had no idea what was going on. She started to get into her sleeping bag, and then she heard it.

There was a cry, as of an animal surprised in its bed. There was scuffling, off in the dark, maybe fifty yards away. It was hard to tell how far away the sound was, in the night, in strange country.

"What's that?" Sally asked Rico.

"I dunno. Listen!"

They heard a soft voice, speaking Spanish. "*Ven aquí, chiquita linda.*" Come to me, pretty little girl. It was Mole calling softly in the night. Another animal cry, softer. A cooing sound came from Mole. "Oh, baby!" he said. *¡Sí, chiquita!* Then after a few minutes came coarse repetitive sounds as though a steam engine was huffing and puffing in the wilderness. It was a voice: "Unh! Unh! Unh!" Another animal cry. Then, piercing the night air, "Unh! Unh! Ahh! Ahh! Rut-rut-rut-rut-rut!"

Sally sat up. "You sons of bitches!" She threw her shoe at Rico, dove into her sleeping bag, and didn't come out 'til morning.

The next morning, after a quick breakfast of coffee and dried scrambled eggs, the trio donned their handguns and prepared to climb the crag. Modesto had his Robar-modified 40-cal Hi-Power, Sally had a Smith & Wesson Model 66, four-inch barrel 357 Mag, and Rico had his new 500 Linebaugh in an old Lawrence 120 holster. Mole was surprised at that choice.

"Rico," he asked, "I thought that cannon was a collector's item. How come you're packin' it?"

"There aren't too many elephants out here, but there *are* grizzlies. Better to be safe than sorry. So I left the Model 29 home and brought this. It needs to get some field time anyway, to be a bona-fide collectible."

They began the climb to the top of the crag. Shortly into the climb they found a cleared trail. "This must be the path the killer used," said Rico. "That's assuming he was up here, and this isn't just some common camp ground used by all and sundry."

"All and sundry? Where'd you go to school?" Sally asked.

"Sorry. I meant to say used by Al and Sandy. You know, casual hikers."

Mole cut in. "Not too many casual hikers out this deep in the bush, Ke-mo sah-bee."

"We shall soon see."

At the top of the crag the trio found a small lean-to made from a camo tarp, set up with a big drop to the front so it looked almost like a tent. It was covered over with brush to hide it from the sky. The brush had been blown and rain-washed from a small part of it, which is why Rico's man Summers found it. The area in front of it had the blackened remains of a fire, and there was some camping gear abandoned there also. Cooking utensils, some powdered eggs, canned goods, a container of water and a light sleeping bag were among the leavings.

After the trio had rummaged through the campsite a while Rico asked, "You guys find anything with someone's name on it? Or any identification at all?"

"Maybe," said Sally. "Take a look at this, guys." She came out from under the lean-to with an object in her blue-gloved hand. It was a folding combination tool, the kind with knife, pliers, saw, screwdrivers, file, can opener, and the like. It had a flat black finish like Parkerizing, and was in a simple case. It had the Gerber name on it.

"That's a Gerber EOD," said Mole. "Military issue. Army engineers use 'em a lot for setting charges, working with C4, stuff like that. Any ID on it?"

"Yes!" Sally said. "There's some initials scratched on it. RCD."

Rico said, "That clears it all up. We're looking for Romeo Charlie Delta. He, or she, might be able to tell us something. Seriously, we might check that for fingerprints." Rico took a close look at it. "Been used a bit."

"You guys hear that?" Mole asked.

A distant whining sound was slowly getting louder.

"Helicopter?" Rico asked. "Kinda early!"

"Doesn't sound right," replied Mole.

"Drone?" asked Sally.

Both men looked at her. "Maybe," said Rico. "The CIA doesn't want us to look into this, so if they're monitoring this area via satellite they may know someone's here. But unless the drone's armed all they can do is look at us, and we're not doing anything illegal."

Sure enough, it was a drone. It came in high from the west, settled into the cleared area, and made a beeline for the top of the crag. It hovered there, as though expecting something.

Unlike colorful drones that take pictures of the naked lady in the shower next door, this one was flat black. It seemed to be inspecting the area to see who, if anyone, was there.

"Who could this be?" asked Sally.

"Most likely CIA," said Rico. They're the ones who want us out of here. I expect they had satellite surveillance on this area to see if anyone came here. Let's just keep out of sight as much as possible behind these trees until it goes away."

"Rico," said Mole, "if it's CIA how do they know there's anything up on top of this crag? They didn't look up here when they came here before."

"Satellite surveillance could have shown them some of our movement in the bushes coming up here. Maybe the smoke from our morning fire." Rico didn't like the situation with the drone hovering so near their location. "We might've set 'em on us our own selves."

"So we showed 'em the way," added Sally. "Now what?"

Rico shook his head. "Wait it out, I suppose. What can they do?"

"I see something on that drone I don't like," put in Modesto. "Looks like a gun."

The drone was large, six or eight feet in diameter. On its front was a prominent camera, and under that was indeed what looked like the barrel of a gun.

CHAPTER 9
Hired

*"*E*ste hombre Lando está muerto. ¿Qué vamos a hacer ahora?"*
"¿Qué pasó?"
"No sé."

In a back room in Caracas Raúl Sanchez spoke with Diosdado Cabello. Cabello is a stocky, somewhat short man with a drastically receding hairline, his gray hair cut short. Second in command to Maduro, Cabello is suspected of serious international drug trafficking, though nothing has been thus far proven. A military man, he wields immense power throughout Venezuela. He is host of a weekly political propaganda TV program called *Con El Mazo Dando*, which roughly means Smack it With a Sledgehammer.

Sanchez told Cabello that Lando Canunny was dead, and they didn't know what to do. In Spanish, they discussed the matter.

"Mr. Lando Canunny was supposed to bring me a *trinket*. Now he's dead. Where's my trinket?" Cabello wrung his hands. "We had a *deal*! In exchange for the trinket I'd arrange to have Mr. Maduro's gold shipped to Canada instead of to Turkey. Canada! And that, despite Canada's having sanctioned me in 2017 for no good reason.

"Mr. Lando was to keep a small bit of the gold for himself for arranging this beneficial deal. Everybody would win! I'd have my gold where I could get it, good cash from it to pay off my street gangs, my daughter would be ecstatic with her jewel, and I'd have the joy of personally handing her that incredible item. Now nobody wins. What in *hell* happened?

"So what do we do now?" Cabello continued. "Is the *trinket* coming with someone else? Is it lost? What's going on?"

"We do not know anything except that this man is dead. He was killed in the wilds of Idaho, a state in the northwestern part of the U.S. Whoever killed him must have the, er, trinket. Because nothing and no one has shown up in over a week we suspect whoever killed him has gone into hiding, perhaps intent on keeping this trinket for himself."

"Can we hire someone to find this killer and recover the, er, trinket? For what's at stake, money is no object." Cabello wrung his hands again. "My poor daughter really wanted to wear this trinket, or one like it, some other big diam..., ah, *trinket* around her neck. I was very much looking forward to giving this special one to her personally, a gift from myself, a token of my love for, and appreciation of my beautiful daughter. We simply must do something to get the item back. It *must* come directly to me!"

Sanchez said, "There is an investigative group, in Idaho as it turns out, that has a history of taking on tough challenges like this one. The group is called 'Boise Control.' Perhaps we can contact them for some help in the matter."

"Are they any good? Any references?"

"Yes! One of the best references imaginable. You recall your friend Juan Cordota y Carazco in northern Mexico? I believe your wife's nephews had dealings with him before they were locked up in the U.S."

"No, I...wait! Wasn't he going to be the supplier of the white substance that got those boys in trouble? I vaguely recall his name now."

"Yes. He is one of the key men in Mexico in the drug trade. He controls much of the cocaine trafficking there and has — fingers — in many things."

"What about him, this Cordota?"

"The gentleman who runs that group in Idaho helped him solve a problem, in a manner of speaking, and Mr. Cordota speaks highly of this American man, one Ricardo Morgan. Morgan is the main agent of the group I mentioned who solve difficult problems."

"Get this Morgan on the telephone, or his handlers, or somebody who knows him, and get him going on this, our problem. Once the diamond, er, *trinket*, is in my hands all will be well and we can finally move the gold. But as much, even more perhaps, than the diamond, we especially want the man who took it, took the trinket. The murdering thief! Of course the thief will have the stone, or know where it is, but I need to get that *hombre*, that *culo* here under my control."

"I'll get right on it," said Sanchez.

"Wait, Raúl. *Momentito*. I think if you hire this Morgan man just to bring us the thief that's all he needs to know. That's better than having him look for the stone, the trinket, and probably easier for him too."

"I will do that. May I ask where is the gold now? Is it safe?"

"*Amigo*, you should perhaps not know this, but it's on the floor of the bay. We put it on board a small vessel and then sank the vessel. To raise it is a matter of piping down some compressed air into some flotation devices, all prearranged, and then we have our gold back. Meantime everyone, including that bastard Erdogan, wonders where it's at."

"You are a clever man. I'll get these Idaho cowboys going as quickly as I can."

"Thank you, Raúl. *Get him now!*"

Two days later I. Yeats Prunzalot was in conference with two other members of the Boise Control team, Kikkan DaKrotch and Eileen Tudarite. Kikkie, as she was known, was brilliant about international politics and Eileen was extremely knowledgeable of financial on-goings in the world. Yeats leaned back in his chair and considered the two women.

"Fair ladies, what do you think of this request from the Maduro regime in Venezuela? Can we accept it?"

"I think Rico would accept it," said Kikkie, "even though the bastard is a dictator. Maduro I mean, not Rico. Although, ya know, Maduro may not stick in Venezuela all that much longer, the way things are going there, with Guaidó trying to move in. But Maduro's money oughta be good, at least as long as he's in power." She drank some tea. "After all, we're just asked to find someone, not actually bring him to justice, or solve three murders. Of course, when we find him we'll most likely have solved them."

"Eileen? What do you think about the finances here, about the money?"

"Historically Venezuela has stashed its jack in Turkey. We see from the news there's a boatload of cash missing. Twenty tons of gold, in fact. They tried to get it out of the country but some sort of embargo was put in place and, presto, the gold disappeared. So that gold is still there somewhere, and Maduro can get at it to pay us — in gold bricks, if it comes to that. We don't know if that pile plays any part in this request to find the killer. What actually did he say, Yeats?"

"Kind ladies, I must bring you up to the date, please. The phone call was from a gentleman by the name of Raúl Sanchez, who mentioned the deceased Mr. Lando Canunny. Mr. Sanchez said that Mr. Canunny was supposed to have met with him in Caracas nearly two weeks ago now. As Mr. Sanchez put it, Mr. Canunny was supposed to be delivering a trinket of some value to Mr. Sanchez, and that trinket was to go to Mr. Diosdado Cabello who would then give it to Cabello's daughter, Daniela. We are not sure why Cabello wanted the trinket or if there was any condition attached to it. Mr. Sanchez did not ask us to recover the trinket, only to find out who killed Mr. Canunny. He offered us a large sum of money if we could deliver the killer to Mr. Sanchez."

"There's your answer, Yeats. The money!" Kikkie crossed her legs and sat back in her chair.

"Eileen, can we trust them for the money?"

"They surely have the money right now," replied Eileen Tudarite. They've got lots of cash in the form of gold, maybe silver, plus guns and other stuff from Russia to the extent of ten billion Russian dollars in so-called aid to Venezuela. And of course that's why Russia wants Maduro to stay in power, because of Russia's huge investment there. So presumably the Maduro people can come up with a substantial payment to us. But I'd suggest we get a significant deposit before saying 'Go!' to Rico."

"Amen to that," added Kikkan. "The way things are going to hell down there Maduro might flee any day to Turkey, or perhaps Russia. Mexico is also a fan of his regime. So whatever we can get in advance may be the only money we'll see."

Yeats passed his hand through his thinning hair. "There's another aspect, my friends. The capture of this murderer ought to bring in some form of reward from the U.S., but so far no one has expressed an interest here in the 'States in his capture."

"Can we look into that, Yeats?" Eileen looked worried.

"Not really. We know he was CIA, but the CIA has asked us to keep out of this completely. So they're not likely to offer us a reward, even if we find the killer. In fact, because of the convoluted way that organization sometimes works, they may not want us to find the killer at all. As you know, Rico and Modesto are, as we speak, indeed looking into the mystery of the murders in the deep mountain forest country of Idaho."

Kikkie sipped her tea, put it down, and asked, "What do they hope to find?"

"Information. There was someone camped there that even the CIA didn't look into. There may be some clues, something left behind that will lead them to some answers."

"I wish them the best. When will they be back?"

"Tomorrow, I'm told." Yeats got up, walked around the meeting room and stared out the window. "If all goes well," he added.

Kikkie leaned forward and put her tea cup on the table. "Yeats, I thought the CIA was not supposed to operate on U.S. soil. What's the deal here? Why are they doing anything?"

"All three of the victims were Canadian born, though Lando Canunny had become a U.S. citizen. They were involved in something that might have begun in Canada. Although we are not yet sure what it was, it would seem that because it *probably* began in Canada and because at least two of them were not U.S. citizens, the CIA is permitted to deal with the matter."

"So are we hired?" Kikkan sipped some more tea.

"I will tell Mr. Rico of the offer and let him know the details, and that we conditionally endorse it. I expect he will say yes, because he is already looking for the killer."

CHAPTER 10
Outrage

"**O**kay, it *is* that bastard Morgan!" Chief of CIA Operations for west Idaho Rip Tibbits spoke to his subordinate Billy Bledsome, who was manning the drone checking out Rico and his friends. "I got a good look at him before he ducked behind that tree."

"You thought it was him when they landed there yesterday. Good call, Chief. Bastard just won't listen. We tole the sumbitch not to meddle, and there he is, meddlin'. Can I shoot him just a little?"

"Yeah, put a few rounds in the ground there, but be sure to not hit anyone. Be a good lesson for him, maybe scare 'im off."

Bledsome put his finger on the firing trigger, and carefully aimed the drone at the ground in front of the trees where the trio were hiding. "What if he shoots back?"

"Shit, he can't hurt it. He might put a few dents in it, but it'd take an elephant rifle to knock out that drone."

"What are we gonna do if that bastard opens fire on us?" Mole was uneasy.

"All three of us are gonna shoot back and see if we can discourage the damned thing." Rico had his big revolver out as he hid behind a stout tree.

A few seconds later a short burst of automatic fire came from the 9mm Uzi mounted on the hovering drone. The bullets tore into the ground in front of the tree where Rico was concealed. Even before the Uzi's echo died away the drone was struck with the bullets from three handguns. The 40-caliber and 357-caliber bullets dented the drone badly near two of the rotors. The smashing 435-grain bullet from Rico's 500 Linebaugh struck the receiver of the drone-mounted Uzi subgun and ripped it half away, off its mount. The muzzle now dangled downward, pointed at the ground. The firing mechanism was destroyed by the shot. The next two bullets from the handguns of Sally and Mole caused more severe denting, but no permanent harm.

Rico pulled the big gun down out of recoil and quickly lined up his second shot on one of the rotors. At the shot the rotor and its motor were torn from the drone. The drone immediately lost all semblance of control and rolled over until it was inverted. The three remaining rotor blades pulled the drone at increasing speed all the hundred and fifty feet to the bottom of the clearing. The CIA drone smashed into the rocky ground and scattered its components far and wide.

Mole spoke. "Well, kids, I suggest we get outa here. If my ears don't deceive me I hear Paul's helicopter coming in. If that's him he's a bit early, thank God." Mole's hearing was right. The trio had enough time before the helicopter landed to descend the hill with some of the camping gear left behind at the campsite on top of the crag. They grabbed their gear from their own campsite, which they'd already packed before climbing the hill to inspect the clandestine camp. Within a few minutes Paul Gobbarander's whirlybird landed and shut down.

"What's that on the ground over there?" Paul asked as they came up to his helicopter. He pointed at the wreckage of the drone at the base of the crag.

"Let's go take a look," suggested Rico. "It was trying to shoot us, but came out second best. There's a gun on it, so be careful on the approach. It might still be active."

The precaution was unnecessary. The Uzi was twenty feet from the wreckage of the drone, its remote firing mechanism smashed by the impact of the heavy bullet from the 500. Rico picked up the gun, made a note of its serial number, and tucked it under his arm. "We don't want to leave this out here," he replied to Paul's raised eyebrows.

Sally found something else. "Rico, look what I found! It's the camera!" She held up a small, expensive-looking device with a lens and battery pack.

"Bring it, dear. It might be of some use to us."

The rest of the drone was smashed to uselessness. They left it as it lay, returned to Paul's helicopter, threw their bags and camping equipment in, and away they all flew, back to Paul's base in North Bedford.

When the helicopter landed at the edge of the field, it was met by none other than the CIA chief for west Idaho, Rip Tibbits. He accosted Rico Morgan with a challenge.

"Morgan, what the hell do you mean by destroying government property? You shot down my drone!"

"What the hell do you mean by shooting at us? We were on public land with every right to be there, and you damned well know it." Rico felt inclined to smack the man, but knew that would be assault, and there were too many witnesses at the little airport.

Tibbits raged. "We were just giving you a warning. We told you to stay out of there and you were meddling in our affairs. It's no concern of yours! Okay, maybe I stepped over the line with you a little. But seriously, there's good reasons for you to keep out of this."

"Why? Because Venezuela's involved and you're planning an overthrow? What else is not new. Or could it be the diamond theft from Canada, and you can't find the stones, and want 'em for yourself?"

"Sumbitch. How'd you hear.... Never mind."

Mole handed the CIA man the battered Uzi recovered from the drone.

"Thanks," said Tibbits. That's one less worry. Tibbits changed the subject. "How in hell did you shoot that thing down, anyway? Elephant rifle?"

"Nope. Just a new little revolver." Rico patted the 500 Linebaugh on his hip.

"What the hell is that? Some kind of cannon?" Tibbits' rage quieted down and his interest in the big revolver took over. What sort of gun could destroy his drone?

"Naw, it's just a common gun. It was just good shooting on my part brought down your bird." Rico smiled to himself as an idea occurred to him.

"What is that, anyway?" Tibbits was curious about the revolver.

"It's a custom Linebaugh five-shot revolver. Wanna shoot it?"

"Hell, yes. I've never heard of a Linebaugh. Come on over to that hill next to the airport and lemme try a round."

"You do much shooting?" Rico asked politely as they walked there. Mole and Sally trailed behind.

"Back a few years I shot some Cowboy Action matches."

"Well, this'll be just your ticket. Poke it out from the hip just like your old six-shooter, let your arm relax, and cut loose at the hillside."

Mole turned his back on Rico and Tibbits. He couldn't keep a straight face. Sally had never fired the gun and had no idea what was going on. She looked at Mole with a slight frown. "Payback time," he whispered.

Rico Morgan and Rip Tibbits walked to within a few yards of the hillside. A small piece of paper fluttered there. Rico unloaded all but the upcoming chamber of the revolver and handed it to Tibbits.

Tibbits gave a cowboy-like glare at the piece of paper, cocked the gun, poked it at the paper from hip height and cut loose. The ferocious recoil of the 500 Linebaugh took the gun upwards and rearwards and smashed it hard into his face. The front sight caught him on the forehead and knocked him unconscious.

Rico reached down, gently retrieved his gun, wiped a drop of blood from the front sight, holstered it, and slowly walked away.

Rico and Mole and Sally drove home across the state in peace. Every so often one of them chuckled.

CHAPTER 11
Egg

"**S**o we've been hired by Venezuela. And you've got a down payment already? Excellent!" Rico, relaxing after the long drive home, got a call from Yeats at Boise Control.

"Actually, kind sir, we were retained by one Raúl Sanchez, as he is the one who sent the retainer to our bank account. He said he represents only Diosdado Cabello, Maduro's right-hand man. He did not specifically say this was an official request from the entire government." Yeats clarified the deal to Rico.

"Okay, Yeats, let's see what we have so far. The killer, whom we're supposed to find, has taken something Sanchez referred to as a *trinket*. Sanchez doesn't want us specifically to find this trinket, but just the guy who took it? We already suspect the trinket was a bag of diamonds, but now, where can this guy be? All we know is his initials might be RCD, that's Romeo Charlie Delta, because of the tool we found at his campsite. He could be anywhere in the world by now."

"I trust you sent the tool to us for fingerprint evaluation?"

"Yes. Shipped yesterday along with a small pillow we found that might have some DNA on it. You can check with NDIS through the FBI. Presumably CIA has records of their agents'

DNA. Now, if we knew exactly what he stole, it might help us find him."

"That is correct, kind sir. That indeedy should help us find him. However, it seems likely, does it not, that he will take the 'trinket' to Venezuela?"

"No. He'd have been there already and we'd be out a job. He's not going to Venezuela. I'd bet a nickel on it."

In a small office at CIA headquarters in Washington, DC, a young blonde agent toyed with her long hair. Roxy Roades was stumped. She had seen it, or rather, *them*, that morning. Going about her daily business she barged into the office of Barbara "Kitty" Katto to deliver a memo, and there sat Jack Marsters, the agent who had accosted Rico and Mole in North Bedford, Idaho. Roxy didn't know Marsters from Adam's off ox, but his presence was not what caught her attention. On the desk of Kitty Katto were three identical odd lumps of rock of a yellowish hue. Each was the size of a hen's egg.

Just as Roxy entered the room, before she saw the stones, Marsters had muttered "...in Canada."

Roxy took a quick look at the rocks on the desk, and asked, "Moon rocks?"

"Miss Roades, please knock before entering my office," Kitty said.

"Never had to before," she replied. In fact you said not to bother if all I was doing was delivering a memo."

"New rules. Thank you, and goodbye."

Roxy went back to her small office, closed the door, and thought about the exchange with Katto. "She didn't want me to see those rocks," said Roxy to herself. "Why not? If not moon rocks, what are they, diamonds in the rough?"

As soon as she said that she gasped, went to her computer, and in the search engine typed in "big diamond." Nothing definitive came up. She sat and thought for a moment, and typed in, "big Canadian diamond." Suddenly her computer screen showed pictures of what was touted as "Giant 552-carat yellow diamond unearthed in Canada's arctic." Another headline read, "Largest known diamond in North America found in Canada."

Roxy was thunderstruck. She had just seen three versions of the newly discovered rough diamond on the desk of Barbara Katto. They were exact copies, it seemed.

It was afternoon now, and Roxy had thought about the rocks all day. She knew the agency had amazing capabilities, but how could it manufacture big, rough diamonds?

"It can't. They're fakes. 'Paste,' they used to be called. But why? Is there some use for them?"

That evening at her home apartment, Roxy turned on the television in a spate of frustration with the world. Her short-time lover Rico Morgan lit up her life for one night, but that was doomed because her good friend Sally Foarth was dating him on a serious level. All the other men she'd dated locally seemed hollow. They were missing something that she desperately needed in her life. But she had no idea what it was. So on went the TV with a wish from Roxy that it might either drown her inner miseries with excessive inanity, or at best — the shining light of a fond hope — entertain her with something worth her time. She poured herself a glass of decent sherry and sat, the TV remote in one hand, the sherry in the other, in front of the tube.

As the picture came on, the TV announcer spat out these words at Roxy:

CARACAS CAPER

"...And to commemorate the recent demise of our beloved cohort, we present to you with all our love, admiration and respect, the final interview performed by Molly Fender for *Fun For Your Life*. We also would like to pay our respects to the late James Fleetwing, another of the recent victims. He was with Molly on this last interview and his image sets the mood of the story. We call this interview, *The Big One*."

The lead-off photo of Molly's last interview was a still shot of the posed image of Jimmy Fleetwing in a tuxedo, holding what looked like a PPK in one hand and the huge yellowish stone in the other hand. He glared out at the TV audience with a ferocious frown on his face from the stylized still image. The James Bond theme music played briefly behind the image.

As soon as Jimmy's image appeared on the screen in his James Bond pose, Roxy gasped. She instantly grasped its significance. Roxy's eyes got big and she stopped breathing. She spilled some of her sherry as she slammed the glass down and turned up the volume.

"O. My. God!"

Half an hour later she was still dazed by what she'd seen and what she'd realized. It was ten in the evening her time. She quickly figured the time out west and began dialing a number on her cell phone. She caught herself, put the cell phone down, grabbed a jacket and dashed out to the nearest small restaurant where she knew there was a public landline phone. She dialed a number in Idaho and shortly was speaking with Rico Morgan on his scrambled phone line.

"Rico, I've got something big for you. I saw the final interview tonight by Molly Fender, the last-ever presentation of her show. I don't suppose you saw it?"

"No. No TV set."

"The leading image for the interview was of Jimmy Fleetwing dressed like James Bond, holding a gun in one hand and this huge diamond in the other."

"The heck you say!"

"And I say more! Today I walked into someone's office at work and there, on her desk, were three copies of the big Canadian diamond. I didn't know what they were, and she chased me out of her office as fast as she could. Wouldn't tell me what the stones were. I went home, thought they looked like quartz or maybe rough diamonds, but...never that big! So I looked up 'big Canadian diamond' and found several photos of what I had just seen on this woman's desk. I came home wondering about it, and then I saw the identical stone in Fleetwing's hand on TV tonight."

"Sonofabitch! They swapped the stone! Jeezus Christ! So that's what they're looking for! Lando was in on this from the start."

"Rico, what do you mean?"

"CIA made, or had someone make, copies of the big stone. Lando left Venezuela, then somehow got his hands on of one of the fake stones and took it to Calgary, where the real stone was. He went there with his sister, Molly Fender, for the interview, and Jimmy Fleetwing went with 'em. Fleetwing used to be a sleight-of-hand artist — ya know, magician type. Christ! Yeats told me that when we first discussed the three victims. I just put it completely out of my mind. Thought it was irrelevant information, but it turns out it was key to the whole thing. Fleetwing got his mitts on the big stone at Calgary, did a quick magical swap, and left behind one of the CIA copies. I'll bet you the ones on the woman's desk were trial runs, maybe not good enough to exactly match the original. Why they kept 'em is another mystery."

"So Lando got the real stone, and he and the others were killed for it. So, where is it now? Any idea?"

"We don't know. No idea whatsoever. No clue. Actually, that's not right. We have some clues and are pursuing them. And I didn't just tell you that. Your CIA buddies can't know that."

"Got it. What else do you know about that stone? Can I ask?"

"We've been hired by Venezuela's Cabello to find the killer. Two weeks ago Lando was supposed to deliver a 'trinket' to Cabello, which means that stone. And now Cabello wants to get in touch with the killer to ultimately get his stone back. I wonder if Lando made some sort of deal with Cabello in exchange for the stone."

"Well, if he did, it must have been in collusion with CIA, because when he left VeeZee to get the stone they *had* to know he was gonna leave, because as you say they got the fake stone to him on his way north. But he wasn't *supposed* to leave, not officially. His job there was not done."

"Hmmm." Rico thought about that. "What if he figured he could leave for a few days, secure the stone, and bring it to Venezuela as part of a CIA deal?"

"Or as part of a side deal?" Roxy frowned. "Maybe not everyone in CIA knew about this deal, is what I'm saying."

"Well, now, slowly it comes out. We'd thought the trio stole a bag of diamonds, or maybe made a deal to bring some drugs or maybe high-tech electronics to the back-woods meet where they got killed. Instead it seems now that they brought that big rock there and were double-crossed. The diamond and the murderer are missing, and for all we know there may have been more than one killer. Our inspection of the camp looked like only one person was there, but maybe not."

"The camp?"

"Yeh. The killer or killers camped a day or two near the murder site before the tragic trio arrived. CIA didn't find that camp, but we did, and went and looked at it."

"Wait! What you said about this killer leaving with the stone meant for VeeZee. If this was a CIA plot, and the stone and thief haven't turned up in two weeks, that means the killer abandoned CIA. Turned rogue. Is a wild card." Roxy chewed on that a while.

"Yes, that's occurred to us too. For your personal information, Roxy, while we were looking at that campsite some asshole at your company named Rip Tibbits sent a drone to shoot at us and we shot it down. He didn't like that."

"My, we do have the adventures, don't we." Roxy chuckled. "Wish I'd been there."

"Wouldn't have worked. Sally was there."

"And you're disappointed with that? Maybe I should tell her. See what she says."

"Why is everybody on at me for a long-ago clandestine meeting with you that, and I quote, 'Never happened!'?"

"I gotta go. Later, Rico."

"Promise?"

After a pause, Roxy answered softly, "Yes!" and hung up.

CHAPTER 12
Killer

The central office of Boise Control was bustling with activity. Although the five main people associated with the group worked only occasionally, and generally out of their homes, all had gathered at the home office of I. Yeats Prunzalot to analyze and discuss all the aspects of this most difficult case, for which they were now hired by a crazy man in Venezuela. The job was to find the man who killed the three visitors to the wilderness clearing in west Idaho, stole a big raw diamond from them, and disappeared.

"Do we have anything at all on the fingerprint report yet, Miss Kikkie?" Yeats, in his thick Indian accent, asked the young Dutch girl who was seated at the main computer terminal.

She responded in her barely discernable Dutch accent, "No Yeats, but it's been promised twice in the last two hours. Just makin' us wait."

"We indeedy found some DNA on that pillow that Mr. Rico sent us. It was a good call on his part to send that along. Now we wait for the FBI to give us something from the National DNA Information System."

Myrtle Stockwood hung up the phone as Yeats was replying. "Yeats, what are the chances of NDIS having anything on this guy? I know he was probably CIA, but would they catalog the DNA of their own people?"

"I would think so," replied Yeats. "In case of a complex situation that might involve the DNA of several people, it would behoove them to be able to tell their people from the other people in such a situation. That is what we are hoping for, at any rate."

G. Willie Kers spoke up in his gruff, cigar-toned voice. "I'm pretty sure they do. I was witness to a situation in Japan a decade ago where a U.S. government man was accused of killing some Japanese car-manufacturer's CEO, or someone close to him. I forget the precise details. There'd been a fight, and there were several types of blood at the death scene, but a check of the DNA at the scene did not match that of the U.S. guy. They didn't need to take his DNA to find out. They had it on file. In that case, 'they' meant international operatives independent of U.S. and Japanese control. They just took the samples, looked 'em up, and cleared the U.S. guy."

"Well, we'll know as soon as the report gets back." Eileen Tudarite sipped her coffee, put it down, and leafed through the sheaf of papers she held. "Nothing here on the make of the pillow or sleeping bag, and nothing on who might have bought that odd tool. I'd guess they issue 'em out of a bulk buy to the various troops. Your tax dollars at work."

"He might'a bought the sleeping bag just for this job, too." Willie frowned at the telephone and desperately tried to make it ring. He was monitoring the NDIS results, which would come in on that phone. He got up and went for a cup of coffee in Yeat's kitchen, adjacent to his home office room, and as soon as he had his hands full of coffee pot and cup, his phone rang. "Aarrghh! Kikkie can you get that?"

"Got it, Willie." Kikkan picked up the landline phone, another of the organization's scrambled, anti-tappable phones. "Hello, BC?" She gave the standard greeting of the organization.

"Is Mr. Kers available?" came the reply.

"One moment, sir." Kikkan covered the phone and called for Willie. "It's your man, Willie."

Kers got the phone. "Kers here. Bill? What do you have, old friend? You do? It was? Excellent! What is it? Spell the last name. Okay, got it. A thousand thanks, Bill."

Willie Kers hung up the phone and addressed the room. "Ladies and gentlemen, we have a winner! Er, make that a loser! Er, I mean, we have the killer! His name is Randy Chancey Didler, ex CIA and now considered a rogue agent. That's the jerk we gotta find."

Yeats responded first. "Brilliant, Mr. Kers! Now, my friends, we have to search the world to find out where this outlaw is. Miss Stockwood, would you please inform Mr. Rico Morgan about this name? Thank you." Myrtle left the room to another secure phone and placed the call. Yeats continued. "What do we know, right now? Anyone?"

Eileen spoke first. "Yeats, all we know for sure is this Didler was last located in the backwoods mountains of west Idaho. No, that's not right. He was last located between there and North Bedford, and might have given up the canoe anywhere before that little town. Most likely he got off at North Bedford, since there are no other towns along the way. So unless he swam many miles out of North Bedford, he would have gone to ground there."

Willie noted, "He could have stolen another boat at North Bedford. Anyone check on that?"

Yeats was on top of that one. "Yes, Mr. Kers. We asked the sheriff if there had been any other boat thefts reported in that little town, and he told us there had not been."

"Could he still be there?" Kikkan asked.

"Possibly, but there are shuttle flights every day between North Bedford and Lewiston, so it's more likely he got out that way. There is a chance that he paid for the shuttle flight with a credit card, because it was an expense he may not have planned on, and he may have been short of ready cash. I will look into that right now." Yeats went to his computer and did the necessary searching and hacking, and in short order told the gathering, "He flew out the day after the murders. So he is indeedy no longer in North Bedford."

"Nuts!" Willie scratched his fast-growing beard stubble. "Too easy. How about we check flights out of Lewiston to maybe get a handle on where he went next?"

Yeats was already busy at his computer. "Give me a few minutes and I may have something." His fingers flew. His brow beetled. He cursed in Indian to himself. "Take a break my friends. This will take a little time."

Myrtle Stockwood, the ex-hooker, made an observation. "If he didn't have cash to pay for that shuttle flight, isn't it likely he used a credit card to pay for wherever he went? Beyond Lewiston, I mean."

"Oh yes indeedy," said Yeats. "I am finding things. Please give me some brief time so I can concentrate fully on this intriguing little problem."

The crew headed for the kitchen. Kikkan DaKrotch walked outside with her coffee to get some air and G. Willie Kers followed her. "Kikkie, what are our chances of finding this galoot? Any thoughts?"

"I think the chances are slim to none, since you asked. He could have stolen a credit card. He may have been issued several under false names by his agency. That would make the most sense."

"I think you're right. So what's the next step?"

"We could use some magic right about now."

Raúl Sanchez was on the phone with Rico Morgan. Rico had phoned him at the number given him by Yeats and quickly made the connection. Sanchez was in a good mood.

"*Señor* Morgan, I appreciate your call. Things are somewhat complex right now here in Venezuela. What can I do for you?"

"Mr. Sanchez, do you have any information concerning the presence in Venezuela of a man named Randy Didler, a U.S. agent, perhaps working with you in the evacuation of your top officials to Mexico, or the preservation of your financial and military resources?" Rico avoided telling him that Didler was the probable killer.

"Do you think this man Didler had anything to do with the death of Lando Canunny?"

"We think an associate of his might have had something to do with it, and that's all we know at this time. We're just following a possible lead." After all, Rico said to himself, we don't *really* know he's the killer, just that he was at the kill site.

"Thank you. I will check with my people and get back to you within the hour." Raúl broke the connection and walked into the adjoining room. "Diosdado, do you recall the name of the American who was chasing your daughter a few weeks ago? He was a good-looking man that seemed to have a decent grasp of Spanish. And your daughter seemed to like him, to the point she put her so-called 'smart' phone down for at least ten minutes to talk with him. Or maybe it was only five minutes."

Diosdado Cabello leaned back in the padded chair in which he sat. "Yes, I recall the fellow. His name was Didler. I told Dani he was a CIA agent and was up to no good. She wouldn't listen to me. No matter what I tell her, she has a mind of her own. The only thing good she does is let me put my messages onto her 'Twitter' site. 'Messages from Daddy,' I think she calls them. All this social media of hers, and what a waste of time it is. All she gets are thousands or millions of horny young men all over the world looking at the photos she takes of herself and then they talk the moon to her, send her messages of 'true love.' 'Oh Dani, how lovely you are. I am a rich Belgian and promise you faithfulness and all my money if you would marry me.' Horse manure. All they want to do is get in her pants. And the same goes for that Didler fellow. I remember hearing the lout saying he'd do anything for her, one day when I should not have been hearing anything. But it was right outside my office they were talking. How could I help but hear? He mooned after her day and night. I think he went off with her to Mexico when our man Lando took her there — and then disappeared. Why do you want to know his name?"

"The man in Idaho, Morgan, wanted to know if Didler had been down here."

"Who?"

"Ricardo Morgan. You know, the head of the group we hired to look for the killer of Mr. Lando Canunny. I thought that young fellow who was chasing after Daniela might have been this Didler person. I must call Morgan and tell him this Didler fellow was indeed down here. That's what he wanted to know."

"Well, at least he's doing something. It's hard to check up on the hired help when they are so far away, no?"

"He did come very highly recommended, you recall."

"¡Verdád!"

Rico hung up the phone. "Mole, I have a slight hunch."

"So did Quasimodo. You know that's dangerous. You gonna go ring some bells? What gives, *amigo*?"

"Diosdado Cabello's man Sanchez just told me Randy Didler was in Venezuela, and was actually chasing after Dani Cabello. There's a good chance, Sanchez said, that Didler went to Mexico with Dani on the same plane that took Lando there. Apparently Didler had hot pants for Daniela."

"*Hombre*, I feel a trip to Mexico might be in the wind."

"*Señor*, you just might be right. By the way, speaking of hot pants, I'm going to Sally's tonight. You've got the house and the cats to yourself."

"*¡Bueno!*"

CHAPTER 13
Mexico

"**A**re you going to...Scarborough Fair?" Rico asked Sally that night in bed. They had enjoyed a simple dinner, and then had great sex afterwards, both of them making up for lost time with each other. They lay now, together in Sally's bed, spent, but not yet sleepy.

"What? Where am I going?"

"Old song. Forgot where you were going with your rusty, trusty fiddle. Was it Timbuktu? South Africa? New Zealand? Melbourne? No! It was Caracas! I remember now."

"No, you don't. I was going to Colombia to approach the border of Venezuela with a symphony orchestra to try to help get the supplies into that country. But now Russia has announced it's sending hundreds of tons of crap directly to Maduro, who continues to lie that the starvation and disease rampant in Venezuela is all a load of hooey and at best a U.S. plot. So if there's no starvation there, why does Russia want to step in with tons and tons of food? That clearly says Venezuela needs the food, and that it's not a U.S. plot. I mean, how stupid is Maduro?"

"He's still in power there and so far as we know there are no options open to kick him out. So that means you're not going?"

"No. The problems at the border essentially made any musical endeavors by us or by any pro-Guaidó government to be pointless. Maduro burned the food given freely by us and several other countries, arrested several journalists who dared contradict him, on and on."

"Yet his man Cabello hired me. It was through Sanchez, but the source was given to me as Cabello. So you think I ought to refuse his money?"

"You forget, Rico, he's a socialist. So the money ain't his. It's someone else's. Probably Putin's, in fact. So by all means take it."

Rico toyed with Sally's breast. "I may have to go to Mexico."

"You may have to go to the hospital if we keep this up all night."

"Seriously, my main suspect is most likely there, with Cabello's daughter, of all people."

"Mole going too?"

"Yes, of course. My Spanish sucks on a good day."

"Why do you think your suspect is hanging out with that girl?"

"They were seen together in Venezuela, and he was goin' nuts for her. He apparently left Venezuela with her, on the same airplane with Lando."

"That's getting cozy. Wasn't Lando after her too?"

"Not certain about that. There was some contact, sure, but there's no way to know what Lando thought of the girl. I mean, he was young and attractive so it's likely, but...head over heels? Doubtful."

"How will you find this guy? The killer. I mean, it's one thing to find Daniela Cabello, whose image and Twitter pictures are all over the place, but do you even know what the killer — what's his name? — looks like?"

"Yes. We acquired good images, Yeats did, of Randy Didler. Interpol, hacked CIA files, and so on. What we'll do is find Daniela and stick close to her. So if our suspected murderer shows up anywhere near Dani we have a good chance of spotting him."

"And then what? Arrest him? On what authority?"

"Yes, arrest him on an international warrant, which we actually have. It originated in Venezuela."

"So you're going to try to find her? And she's attractive? Might want to take me along to chaperone you."

"Seriously I'd like some bona fide U.S. agent to go along too, in case we come up against international laws or Mexican legal prerogative of one sort or another, and can't get him out of Mexico."

"Rico, say this Didler fellow has the diamond. What's he going to do with it? He can't exactly peddle it, can he?"

"My guess is he gives it to Dani to get in her pants."

"Can you get it back from her?"

"Not my job. In fact, if she has it and makes it known, and her dad finds out, I'm most likely out of a job. All we'll get is the down payment we already have. Unless, of course, they want Didler over and above the big rough diamond."

"So why go after him? Why not just tell Sanchez or Cabello that Didler is in Mexico, and we can go play in the woods?"

"Honor, I guess. Reputation. We're being paid to find the killer and do what we can to apprehend him. That sort of follow-through is why I'm still in business. Also, I suspect things are so tight in Venezuela now with Guaidó trying to roust Maduro that they can't spare any people to go to Mexico to get Didler."

"Okay. So can we go to sleep now?"

"Not...quite...yet." Rico came closer to Sally, and she came closer to him. Things progressed, Rico managed — barely, as he later said — to stay out of the hospital, and the two lovers had another happy time and then a good night's rest.

"Rico, we've gotta go right now!" The next morning back home Rico was suddenly confronted by Modesto Pincata Buena over late-morning coffee.

"What's the rush?"

"Take a look at this photo Kikkan sent over. This came off of Dani's Twitter page yesterday." The photo showed Daniela at a ball of some sort, with several of her lady friends next to her. On the right side of the photo, nearly out of the frame, was the clearly discernable face of Randy Didler.

"Where was this taken? Yeats know yet?"

"Mexico City, at the ball for celebrating the birth of some ancient socialist mediary. The hall where it was given is the 'Home for Retired Mexican Veterans,' loosely translated. That's in the west-central portion of the city."

"So he was there. When?"

"Two days ago."

"Did Yeats and the team get any more info?"

"Not yet," Mole replied. "It's a rare thing for anything pertaining to Daniela herself to be posted on her Twitter site. Most of it is Maduro or Daniela's father spouting endless propaganda."

Rico went to the window and looked at the apple tree in the yard. "So how are we to find one person among twenty million others?"

"Like the guy with the whip, at least for right now."

Two days later Mole and Rico stepped off the airplane in Mexico City, rented a car, drove to a reasonably priced hotel near the west side of the city that Myrtle Stockwood recommended, and checked in. Yeats had made their reservations in advance. In their hotel room the two took stock of what they had.

"Thanks to Yeats's hacking and Kikkan's political savvy we have a potential address for the queen of the Cabello family." Rico gave a copy of the address to Mole. "Yeats put it on my iPad Air-2 map unit, so it ought to be easy to find. The only guns we have are the two Kel-Tec P3AT's we brought, in the special luggage-hideout boxes. I guess 380s are better than nothing."

"We could maybe buy some bigger guns here, but do you think we'll need 'em?"

"We're gonna try to bring this Didler to justice. I'd bet he has a bigger gun, and more than just one. How about we buy shotguns?"

"That might be a good idea, amigo." Mole wiped the last bit of oil off the tiny pistol and pocketed it in his jacket. Inside the jacket pocket was a sort of stiffener or holster so the shape of the gun could not be seen casually.

"What say we go scope out this so-called residence of Dani's and see what we're up against? We can take a jug of coffee and some snacks and see if we get lucky." Rico pocketed his own 380.

"*Bueno. Vámonos.*"

Mole drove them in the rental car out the Paseo de la Reforma and bore west into the heart of the wealthy section of the enormous city. Rico observed, "Of all the cities in all the world, this is the one to go to if you want to become lost. A guy could just slip into the poor section, any of these barrios, and *zip*, gone forever."

"Not so, *amigo*. The people who live in the barrios are extremely street-wise and know who belongs there and who does not. An outsider would be known to everyone in a couple hours. Trust me on that. I grew up there. Better to dress like a tourist and wander the medium- to high-dollar areas."

"What if our boy don't spikka da Spanich?"

"Not a big problem for him. Most of the cops speak English, and all of the vendors do, especially the high-dollar ones who want the U.S. dollars."

"Do we expect our girl to associate with high-visibility people here? I'd guess yes."

"*¡Seguro!*" In his native land, in his native city, Modesto Pincata Buena increasingly reverted to his native tongue. "She'll hang out with TV and movie stars, go to all the high-dollar pubs and bars, dance the night away with the wealthy gigolos, all to get more pictures of herself for Twitter or Instagram."

"Her Instagram account's been blocked. So it's Twitter or nothing. We can only hope that account stays current so we can keep up with her social wanderings."

"How close are we?" Mole asked, as they drove along.

"The GPS map-finder on the Air-2 sez make a right turn at the next crossroads, head north for a mile, turn left, and go what looks like a hundred yards. We must be ten miles out from the city."

"*Solamente ocho*, only about eight, as I recall." Mole took the right turn, followed the road per Rico's instructions, and in short order they arrived at their destination, the house in which Daniela Cabello was reportedly staying.

The house was, like so many in Mexico City, surrounded by a wall with glass on top of the wall. The barred iron gate was automatic, with no guards in sight. All they could see of the house was through that gate, except for the upper stories of the house that were higher than the wall. There were trees within, lots of other greenery, and the middle levels of the house had balconies that looked over the yard. The balconies could not see the street except through the barred gate.

Mole drove slowly by the front of the house. He took the car down the street half a mile, turned it around, and returned to within two hundred yards of the gate, parked at what passed for a kerb, and shut off the engine. There were no buildings on the side of the street where they parked, just a sort of grassy park that ran off to trees. In the far distance other fancy, walled dwellings were visible above and beyond the trees. A few cars lined the road where Mole parked, the riders of some of them enjoying the grassy park. Others were perhaps visitors to some of the walled houses on the other side of the street. In the distance across the grass a couple had a picnic rug on the ground in the shade of some trees. Two men sat at one of the many park benches under a tree in the near distance and drank what appeared to be beer. A few people walked dogs. A young couple held hands and enjoyed a walk in the park in the warm afternoon.

"Now we wait," Mole said. There's nothing else to do.

"Any ideas what to do if we see him?" Rico settled himself in the seat for a long observation session, reached down to the floor and picked up a large bag that held numerous things to eat and drink, including a thermos of coffee, cleverly put together by Mole before they left their hotel. Rico pulled a set of Leitz 8X32 Trinovid field glasses out of the bag and put the binocular where they could easily get at it.

"We could try to arrest him, but chances are he won't be alone. There's gotta be guards for this girl and she and the guards will most likely go with Didler if they go anywhere."

"Shit. This is like something out of a Spenser novel. That poor bastard spent half his life waiting for stuff to happen while he was on stakeout." Rico poured coffee.

"Welcome to the club, *amigo*." Mole accepted a paper cup of coffee and slouched down in the seat like Rico, making himself less noticeable. The weather was warm but comfortable. It was the middle of the afternoon when they settled in.

CHAPTER 14
Stakeout

As afternoon became twilight the two men alternately nodded off, taking turns keeping an eye on the entrance to the residence where they believed Daniela Cabello was currently residing in Mexico City. Rico Morgan was asleep in the passenger seat, and Modesto Pincata Buena slouched behind the steering wheel, the binocular in his hand. With a groan and curse, Rico woke up.

"Anything new, Mole?"

"Yeah. You remember the two guys having beer under yonder tree? They've gone away, but there are two more guys there. Guess who they are."

"I have no idea...oh Christ! I bet it's the CIA goons from west Idaho, I'll bet a nickel."

"You win the nickel, *amigo*. We knew they'd be looking for this guy and figured it all out, just like we did."

"They spot us?"

"Probably. They're trained to use their eyes and we've sat here hours without leaving the car except to pee in that public bathroom behind us. They don't have spy glasses, and they're so close to the gate they don't need 'em. But they'd surely be suspicious about us."

"We could go play Frisbee in the park. Throw 'em off the track." Rico looked worried.

"What if we went to talk with 'em. Tell 'em we're not after the diamond, just the guy."

"I doubt they'd believe us, Mole."

"We could go shoot 'em."

"Naw. Too much noise in this quiet neighborhood. And then there's the bodies."

Twilight settled in and became darkness. Lights were on all up and down the street. No one came out of the target household. The night crept on. The two men on the park bench gave up. Rico and Mole gave up.

"No one coming out tonight. We shoulda figgered that, it being Thursday night. Mole, what say we go home, get some beans, and try again tomorrow."

"*Bueno.*" Mole started the car and took the two heroes back to their hotel.

Over dinner that night the men discussed the situation. Rico was disgusted. "*Amigo*, there's no sense in our sitting there day after day. Is there a way we can get them to come out? Or some way we can go in?"

"There's a good chance they'll go out on the town tomorrow night, as it's Friday. I say let's get there mid-to-late afternoon, and give it a shot. If they don't, we could maybe set the place on fire. Or set off a bomb in their back yard."

"Okay, Mole, but let's go over the plan again if they do come out. I still think we might want to try to nab 'em there at the gate, but of course they'll have guards surrounding her. We can't just shoot 'em all."

"No, we can't shoot any of 'em unless they shoot at us first. Even then we'd have to explain ourselves to the *policia* when they come."

"Rico, look here in the paper!" The next morning the two were having coffee in the hotel room. "This fellow is playing tonight! His name is Chayanne, he's a singer, and he has a Venezuelan wife. I'll bet a nickel our Dani will go to see him. They may even know each other; I mean this guy's wife, who used to be a beauty queen in VeeZee, and Daniela."

"Where is he performing?"

"That's the key to this. The concert hall, *Auditorio Nacional*, is not two miles from that house where Daniela is staying. It seems like that'd be the place for them to go tonight."

"Can we work our plan there?"

"I think so. There'll be crowds outside, up and down and all over the vast stairs there, more in the lobby, and even in the main room before the performance begins. We should be able to get right up to him easily that way. Dani's guards might be there, but they won't be able to bring out the Uzis or MP5's, whatever they've got under their coats in such a crowd. If they do, they can't shoot without killing dozens of people. We should be able to sidle up to Randy and take him with no fuss."

"Okay, works for me. I just want to get out of this country with our hides intact."

From her home in east Idaho Sally Foarth called Tom Dickannary, her NSA contact in DC. "Tom, I think I need help. Rico and Modesto are in Mexico going after Randy Didler, the presumed killer of the trio in the back country here in Idaho. Didler was seen with Daniela Cabello in Mexico City. Is there any way we can keep track of Rico and Modesto, or maybe send someone to help 'em out? It's just the two of them and undoubtedly Dani Cabello has armed guards surrounding her."

"Back up, Sally. What exactly are they there for? Why are they in Mexico City?"

"Sorry, Tom. Of course you don't know. Rico was hired to arrest Randy Didler by a foreign, er, diplomat. Didler stole the big Canadian diamond and disappeared, but was seen recently in Mexico City in the company of Daniela Cabello, the daughter of Venezuelan Vice-President Diosdado Cabello. So Rico and his friend went there to see if they can arrest this guy."

"Good luck to them. How do they expect to get past the armed guard of the girl to get at the guy?"

"Rico and his friend said they have a plan, but I don't know what it is. I was hoping we could send one of our people there, or perhaps someone in CIA because CIA is already after this guy too. I know of only one operative in CIA who might work, because she knows Rico."

"NSA won't get actively involved, and of course you can't go, for several reasons. Since the orchestra arrangement washed out there's really no need for you to get anywhere near Venezuela, and going to Mexico is also out because your friends don't know you're NSA, you don't speak Spanish well, and because you're close enough to Rico Morgan that it would, or could, present compromises and danger to you both."

"You mean we'd look out for each other too much instead of concentrating on the target. I understand, Tom, which is why I called you. And I don't want him to know I'm in this agency."

"I don't know if we can persuade CIA to send anyone else, even a specific person who knows Morgan. I'll look into it and get back to you later today."

"Thanks, Tom." Sally broke the connection and went back to her daily violin practice.

Later that afternoon Sally got a phone call. She was sure it was Tom about to reject her request. She was wrong.

"Sally, it's Roxy. I hear you want someone to watch out for a couple of bums in Mexico City for you."

"Roxy! Yes, well, I though it'd be a good idea to have someone else down there to watch their behinds, help them in time of need when they run out of ammo, maybe even absorb all the bullets that get shot at them. Can your agency spare someone like that?"

"Yes. Me. I've been detailed to go there to watch them, keep a clandestine eye on a quartet of our own guys, and maybe help whomever I can help, as the need arises."

"Wow! If you try absorbing all those bullets, be sure to wear a bulletproof vest. Are you coming here first? Or going directly to Mexico City?"

"I'll be flying direct to Mexico City tomorrow out of Detroit Metro. I'm in western Michigan right now. I wanted to have some work done to my Centennial Airweight and also to my hideout PPK, so I came to a specialist gunsmith shop here, a place called Michiguns. The owner, Ned Christiansen, is a brilliant workman. He did some work for a few of the guys I work with, and I liked what I saw. This guy's got a backlog of, like, eight or ten years, but he went out of his way to help me. He knows Rico, so he's doing a rush job on my PPK, putting some kind of kinky pyramids on the grip strap. He also found a few glitches in the innards of my revolver, so he's making that right too, and slicking up the pull. Rico knows the darnedest people. "

"Is this gunsmith good looking?"

"He's pretty much okay, but he's married, so no dating or anything. Nice guy, anyway. His kid's a real whiz."

"Well I hope you can do the boys some good down there. Do you know where they are?"

"I have their hotel information from Yeats at Boise Control. I asked him to say nothing to Rico. Better he doesn't know I'm coming. It might be a good idea to keep in the background for a while."

"Excellent, my friend. Please give my regards to Rico if and when you do see him, but don't tell him I wanted someone to go protect him. He'd probably cry."

"Okay, Sally. You playing any concerts? Anything coming up?"

Sally told Roxy about the cancelled Venezuela-benefit concert in Colombia. "There's nothing else on the books right now, but the Denver Phil wants me to headline a concert there late summer or early fall. Me or Xiao Liu. Ditto a group in Oregon, and a third in Ann Arbor, again this fall. The Brits want me back too, but I won't go there until at least next year. Always something coming up."

'Take care, Sally, and keep your fiddle in tune and my agency in mind."

"You bet. Watch yourself down there."

"Always."

CHAPTER 15
Concert

Friday's late afternoon found Rico and Mole in the car again, watching the residence that housed Daniela Cabello. "Rico, there ought to be a better way to do this than just sittin' here. How about a tiny remote-controlled camera with a zoom lens concealed in a tree, or fence post, or even on a car top. This thing could be sending images by means of WiFi or some similar broadcast technology to a computer screen hundreds of yards away, or hidden inside a van. I know this technology exists. All we'd have to do is watch the screen instead of sitting in the car like a couple of dumbos. Back a few years, that TV show *She Spies* had a setup like that. The surveillance van, they called it. I know it was fake, but after, what, fifteen years the technology must be out there."

"Yep. All it takes is flying in a special van with all that stuff inside, or driving down from Texas or New Mexico with it, and several months to plan it all. And then who's going to pay for it? Not me, baby."

"I'll be quiet now."

"There they go!" Twilight was upon them as the gate to the house opened and a big car drove out. It was a black Mercedes limousine. The tinted windows gave no clue as to who was inside.

"They may not be in there, but how many limo's would they have, and why would Dani stay home on a Friday night?" Mole cranked up the car and began to follow the limo.

"Let's go find out!"

As expected the Mercedes limo headed in the direction of the *Auditorio Nacional*, but about a mile before they got there the limo pulled over to the kerb near a convenience store and a man got in. As Mole drove past the parked limo the street light showed the man to be Randy Didler. Mole pulled over discretely, let the limo go ahead again, and the two cars, separated by a quarter mile, drove to the *Auditorio Nacional*.

"Rico, he don't live with her. What do we do if we lose him?"

"I guess we keep on following her. Where she goes he goes. Unless you have a better idea?"

"Let's see how things go tonight at the auditorium."

They parked the car not far from the limo and saw the bright red dress that Dani was wearing as she got out with Didler. She stood out strikingly from most of the crowd. Randy Didler emerged from the limo in a dark gray suit, which could easily blend into the crowd of several thousand people lining the great steps and street in front of the music hall.

"Mole, let's take him now." Rico and Mole moved closer to the odd couple.

As they drew near to Dani and Randy, two men came out of the crowd and intercepted Rico and Mole. They were Billy Bledsome and Jack Marsters, the two CIA goons that had been in Sheriff Lutz's office in North Bedford, Idaho.

"Hold it right there, asshole." Bledsome spoke. "We know exactly how to do this and we want you to stay out of it."

"What about the guards, whom you don't see and didn't evaluate?" Rico asked him.

"You're wrong and I'm right and I don't care what you say. There ain't no guards. Watch us, stupid. We're lots smarter than you." Bledsome gave Rico and Mole a half-concealed smirk.

Daniela turned toward the sound of the rough English language spoken so close to her. As she did, Rico and Mole saw that Daniela was wearing the huge uncut Canadian diamond in a gold setting around her neck.

Bledsome and Marsters joined two other men and approached Daniela Cabello. As they got close to her and made to stop her, Dani's five guards appeared out of the surrounding crowd with guns drawn. At that moment Mole said to Rico, "Get lost!" and tossed the car keys to him. Then Mole said something in rapid Spanish to Daniela, addressing her as Dani.

Bledsome ignored the guards and whatever they were saying in rapid-fire Spanish, and reached for Daniela. As Bledsome reached for Dani he said to Randy, "Didler you're under arrest." As Bledsome's hand went to Dani's shoulder and his other hand disappeared into his jacket, five shots rang out. Bledsome took two in the head and three in the body and collapsed on the spot.

Mass hysteria took over the crowd closest to the group. A girl fainted, several screamed, and they all rapidly oozed away from the little group that held the dead man, Rico, Mole, Dani and her guards. The other three CIA men faded into the crowd, showing a lot more sense than Bledsome had shown.

"So much for being right, and smarter than us," said Rico. He got no response from Mole. Rico looked for Didler but didn't see him.

"Where'd he go?" Rico looked all around but could not spot Randy Didler anywhere. "Mole, where'd *you* go?"

When Mole didn't answer, Rico looked for him and to his utter surprise Mole was walking arm in arm with Daniela toward the music auditorium. One of the guards was with them, but the other four melted into the crowd and disappeared. Rico quickly disappeared into the crowd heading toward the music hall. All that was left of the night's havoc was the dead man on the ground.

"Wait," Rico said to himself. "I'm not going in there. Mole's obviously okay, so why don't I try to find Randy. That's what we came for." This ran through Rico's head as he neared the door of the auditorium. He slipped over to the left, around the huge grand-entry pillar there, past some outdoor benches next to the small potted trees at the side of the entrance, and then down all twenty-five stone steps to the left side of the auditorium. This was the opposite direction from where the dead man lay, over by a huge bronze statue at the other end of the main entrance. By roundabout means Rico found their rental car, got in it, and sat for a spell.

"Okay, I know we came down the Paseo de la Reforma, but did they pick up Randy before then? Or along that main drag? Where could he be? I wish someone would come and show me the way."

Rico nearly wet himself as someone tapped on the driver's window just then. A woman in casual evening wear stood there. He rolled down the window, looked at her, and nearly wet himself again. It was Roxy Roades.

"Waba dabba? Fum linga puppa?" Rico seemed to have lost control of his tongue.

"Same to you, Mister Morgan. Can I get in, or do I have to stand here all night?"

Rico got out of the car, made to go to the other side to open the door for her, then turned and took Roxy in his arms. The former lovers embraced, and then leaned back in each other's arms to look at each other.

"Roxy, I'm so glad to see you. What are you doing here?"

"Decided to come down for a vacation, saw you in the crowd, and thought you might need someone to look after you. Where's Mole?"

"That's a load of crap and I know it. I saw four of your buddies tonight already, but one got whacked by Daniela Cabello's overanxious bodyguards. He's still lying over there on the ground. Are you with them?"

"No. I saw the shooting. Stupid Bledsome asked for it. Where's Mole she asked for the second time," said Roxy. "Don't bee-ess me, Ricardo Morgan."

"Er...he was last seen entering the concert hall with Daniela Cabello on his hairy arm. He tossed the keys to me just before the shooting and told me to get lost. We both got dressed reasonably for this concert in case we had to blend in with the crowd. Mole looked entirely appropriate to have Dani on his arm. He probably knew what was gonna happen because of his, you know, understanding Spanish and all. He said something to Daniela just before all hell broke loose with the guards, and next he's escorting Dani into the concert just like nothing happened."

"Does she have the diamond?" Roxy asked.

"Yes, but we're not after it. All we want is the guy who was her escort, one Randy Didler. He disappeared right after the shooting, so Daniela had no proper escort. As I think about it, Mole's actions prevented her getting arrested or detained.

"Why couldn't one of the guards become her escort?"

The guards are pretty much dressed like goons, not like concert goers."

"Goons?"

"Crappy loose clothes. One guy had patches on his sleeves, they all had tattered trousers, bush coats, dirty scuffed shoes. Two had dress jackets. One of them went with Mole and Dani. But they all had good guns. Two looked like MP-443s, Russian Grachs. The others were Makarovs. Probably all of those guns were provided to Venezuela by Putin. How'd you find me, anyway?"

"I saw this singer Chayanne was playing here tonight. He's really popular among Latinos, so if Dani was going anywhere tonight she'd come here. He kinda looks like Mole, in fact. So rather than beat on your hotel-room door I came here expecting to find you on her tail. I was right."

"Good work! I don't understand how the CIA guys all convened here. They were on stakeout with us yesterday but not today. They must have figured she'd come here, just like you did, Roxy."

"Actually I suspect they snuck something into her house to listen in. Some sort of bug which let them overhear her plans for tonight. So they just came here instead of staking out her residence and following her...just like some dummy out of an old Spenser novel. So what's your plan, Spenser?"

"Ain't got one. We were going to nab Randy Didler here but got overruled by the CIA. Randy ran, and I don't know where."

Unlike his preference at home, Rico carried a cell phone in Mexico. It rattled in his pocket. "Yes?" he answered.

"Five twenty-one West Reformánce street, second story." It was Mole and that's all he said before he broke the connection.

Rico repeated it to Roxy. "I suggest we go there. I have no idea where it is, but my iPad Air-2 might show it." He plugged the address into his navigation program and the device indicated approximately the place where the Mercedes limo picked up Didler on its way to the auditorium. "I suspect Mole got this info out of Dani somehow. She'd know the address because she installed Didler there when they first came to Mexico City."

"Are you armed?" Roxy asked.

"I've got a tiny 380 we managed to sneak in. Mole has one too. What about you?"

"I've got my PPK with its nifty new grip."

"How'd you get that in?"

"I work for the government. You don't. I was given all the necessary paperwork to get the gun into and out of Mexico with the least trouble. So, let's go get this guy."

CHAPTER 16
Chase

Rico and Roxy drove to the address that Mole had given them, following Rico's GPS program on his iPad Air-2. At that address was a sort of convenience store, but it appeared to have apartments above it. A flight of stairs behind an iron gate to the right of the shop led upward. The two saw all this from a slow drive-by. They turned around and, essentially staking it out, parked fifty yards from the gated entrance to the stairway.

"He's probably walking, and it's nearly a mile, so we may see him arrive here if we're lucky." Rico settled down in the car.

Roxy turned slightly in the seat to face Rico. "Is there a reason for him to come here? Might he not try to sneak into the music hall and join up with Dani?"

"Doubtful. He knows CIA's after him now, hot on his trail. The three remaining CIA guys'll surely keep an eye on her. One of them, Marsters, knows who Mole is, but they probably don't know we're not after the diamond. If that's the case they may get stupid again, but I doubt they'd risk it with all those people in the main auditorium. They might try for her or the diamond if there's an intermission, but again it wouldn't be smart. Not with her trigger-happy guards sticking to her. Whadda you think, Rox?"

"My guess is the CIA guys will fall back, make new plans, maybe even leave the country since they now know where the stone is. I suspect Randy's a distant second place in their plans. Sure, he's a rogue agent, but they don't really care. He's no threat anymore to anyone."

"The only thing keeping Didler in this country, in this city, is the girl. He must've scored big-time by handing her the stone. I was really surprised he was not staying with her at that walled house."

"She's the guest of someone, and whoever that is might not like the idea of cohabitation, believe it or not. These people, a lot of them, especially the ones with the money, might act like liberals, but they're really extremely conservative, especially concerning old-school values."

"I wonder if he even got in her pants."

Roxy thought about that for a long beat. "Could it be, Rico, that he just wanted to get in good with her father? With the Maduro regime?"

"Whoa. Mebbe. Good point. All along we've assumed he wanted to get next to her. Word from Cabello through his man Sanchez was that Lando Canunny and Dani were tight. He also indicated Didler was going nuts over her. So if that was the case, and we still assume it is, Daniela might have rejected Didler for some reason, took the stone, said thank you very much, now go diddle yourself."

"So he killed three people for nothing." Roxy stared out the windshield down the empty street.

"Yep. Looks that way. No love from Dani, no stone to bargain with any more."

"If that's the case there's no reason for him to stick around. He might try to get the stone back, but then, that's what the late Mr. Bledsome did, and look what it got him."

"Yep."

"Let's say we're right." Roxy was on a roll and Rico let her roll. "Didler's maybe — or maybe not — gonna come here and gather up his...stuff. Whatever he has stashed up there. Maybe money, clothes, who knows. Then where's he going? Not the U.S. because he's wanted for murder there. We don't know if he speaks Spanish but probably not. He might go to Colombia and try to get into Venezuela. But can he fly there? Or would he drive? If he comes here...."

Rico cut in when Roxy paused. "What if we botch getting him. He runs. Where's he go? Airport to get out of Dodge? First flight to Anywhere-Inna-World? Or would he rent a car, or steal one, and head south?"

"Here's one for you, Mr. Morgan. What if we *do* get him? What do we do with him? Tie him up for the night until you collect Mole, then fly him to Venezuela? What if he shoots one of you? Do you have any authority to shoot back?"

"We have an international arrest warrant from Venezuela, which Mexico should honor. Dunno about Colombia, but most likely they will. So we could throw him in a local pokey on that warrant, which would keep him until we're ready to fly him to Venezuela. Or even better, we inform our man in VeeZee who then sends troops or cops or goons to come get him. They pay me, we fly home and drink. A lot. We'll drink a lot. Y'know, good booze."

"I have nothing to help you. I'm here unofficially. I have zero authority to do anything. All I can do is shoot back if anyone tries to nail us." Roxy patted her belt, where her loose top covered the holstered gun.

"You can help. What say we walk slowly down the street toward the gate, like we were going to the convenience store. We can hold hands like we're on a date and not draw any attention to ourselves. Then when he comes, we put gun to his head, slap on the cuffs..."

"Have you got cuffs?"

"Yes. Once we have him cuffed we take him to the local slammer and go home and wait for Mole to join us. Or phone us."

"Let's do it!"

The two got out of the rental car and put the simple plan into action. They walked slowly toward the convenience store, the near side of which had the gate to the stairs. As they walked they saw a man coming toward them, walking rapidly.

"Here he is. I'll slap a gun to his head," said Rico, and you can cuff him. If he struggles I'll try to take him alive. We don't need any guff from the local police tonight. Does he know you at all?"

"No. I don't think so. I hope not. Anyway, we're just two Latin lovers strolling down the lane on a Friday night."

The man approached, passed them on the outside and as he did Rico put his hand on the man's arm and his P3AT to the man's head and said, softly, "Randy, don't move." Roxy came around and put her gun to the man's back and felt for a gun. Randy didn't move. He knew the score and played it smart. Roxy found a tiny Browning 25 auto and a one-hand knife.

In a few seconds they had the cuffs on him and Rico said, "Randy C. Didler, you're under arrest by an agent of the Venezuelan constituency. You'll be transported to a local slammer tonight and flown to Caracas tomorrow. Do you have any questions?"

Silence.

Rico and Roxy got him in their car, found the nearest police station, and after an hour of explanations and multiple readings by the local law people of Rico's arrest warrant from

Venezuela, signed by Cabello and Sanchez and other worthies in the Venezuelan political scene, they got Randy Didler behind bars. Rico told the local gendarme they'd be in the next day to escort the prisoner on down the road to his destiny in Caracas.

Later, in his hotel room, Rico sat with Roxy waiting for a call or some contact from Mole. It was approaching midnight and they had heard nothing.

"Rico, I'd better get me a room because I don't yet have one."

"You could stay here. No hanky and no panky. Just convenience and expeditiousness. You can sleep in Mole's bed or, if you prefer, mine, and I'll sleep in his."

"Okay," she said. "That makes things a lot easier."

Earlier they had had a simple bit of food sent up and also a bottle of decent white wine. Some of the wine remained and they each had half a glass as they sat in the room with the TV on but silent. Roxy thought it would be a good idea to watch it for news of the shooting earlier that night. Nothing was reported on the late TV news about it.

Rico snapped off the TV after the news report and said, "I wonder if the other CIA guys took the body away before any local police showed up."

"Even if they did, there'd be enough people there to say something to someone about it. These folks all have smart phones and all it would take is the Mexican equivalent of nine-one-one by any one of 'em to bring the cops."

"So the cops show up, find a dead body and no one claiming it? Wouldn't they go inside, stop the concert and ask?"

"Rico, this is Mexico, and the richest part of Mexico City. I'd guess they do things a little more discretely here, especially if Bledsome had ID on him, and the cops find out he's American. If they find out he's CIA they'd try to keep it quiet, I'd guess. So we may never hear or see anything more about that shooting on the TV or elsewhere."

Rico's cell phone rang. He grabbed the unit and saw it was Modesto. "Mole, where are you?"

"I'm in the house we staked out. Got only a few seconds. I won't be in tonight. Will see you tomorrow."

"We have Randy in jail."

"We? Who's we?"

"Roxy showed up."

"Ah! Good work. How are her pants?"

"See you tomorrow at the hotel."

"¡Claro! Good luck tonight."

"Bite me." Rico broke the connection.

Roxy sipped her wine. "What was that all about? Why do you want him to bite you?"

"He made a rude comment about you and I together."

"Does he know? About...us, before?"

"No. He guesses, but no one knows for sure but we two."

"Rico I wish we could have had more. It was sooo good."

"As Mole would say, ¡Claro que sí!"

Silence fell over the room as the two former lovers drank wine alone in the hotel room deep in the heart of Mexico City.

"Rico, I'm going to get a shower."

"I just thought of something. Where's your bag? What'd you bring that we need to go get?"

"Just this small bag. I tossed it in your car when I first saw you." It was about the size of a thick briefcase with a shoulder strap. Rico had thought it was just a big purse. "It's got all I need."

"Okay. If you need anything just holler and I'll go get it. The hotel has a lot of stuff for sale in the lobby for the tourists...like us, I guess. I'll get a shower after you do."

"Or you could join me...."

Rico gently put his wine glass down, stood up, and took her in his arms. They kissed like the lovers they were, full of passion and pent-up energy. The kiss lasted as they both stripped, lasted until they fell on the bed together. They took each other, joined, released, joined again in writhing passion. To each of them it seemed like they had never given up wanting each other, not since their one night together long months ago. Their passion became blind lust for each other's body. They tasted, touched, gripped, clung together and came apart, looking deeply into each other's eyes. Rico slowly slid into Roxy, and she rose to meet him. They joined, fully, and then were pumping, thrusting, grinding against each other until with loud cries the lovers climaxed together.

After their first joining they lay together on the bed, toying with each other's body, kissing, breathing each other in. Then came more searching, continued needs. They came to each other again and again, and enjoyed each other fully.

Later, as they lay together, fully spent, Rico broke the silence of the night. "It's a good thing my girlfriend doesn't know you're down here."

Roxy giggled. "She sent me, Rico."

"Aarrghh!" he cried, and sat up in bed. "Are you trying to get me killed?"

"No, I'm here to keep you alive, doing whatever it takes. Now, at least, we won't be both wishing we were in bed together instead of dodging bullets."

Rico had nothing to say to that. A little later they showered together and went to bed to sleep.

CHAPTER 17
Randy

Randy Didler was unhappy. Lying on the bunk in his jail cell in Mexico City, he looked back at what had happened in the preceding weeks. The CIA sent him down to Venezuela with a few other men and women, one of whom was Lando Canunny. Randy knew him slightly from a previous job. Their job in Venezuela was to help save, extract, or if necessary destroy things that the Maduro regime might want to take with them that they really ought not to have, such as ultra-high-tech weapons from Russia. Especially, the CIA was there to help evacuate high-ranking political personnel from the country before anyone, officially or otherwise, ousted Nicolás Maduro. In the course of this work Randy Didler met Daniela Cabello, and that was the start of his trouble.

Randy fell, hook line and sinker, for Dani. He would do anything, *anything*, for her. One unhappy day the young CIA agent overheard her talking with her father, Diosdado Cabello. He understood enough Spanish that he could make out what they were saying, though he could not speak much of that language. He heard her say she wished some knight-errant would come along and give her a huge diamond and carry her off to a big castle, away from all the so-called social media and false people so that she never again would have to deal with all the phonies who came along and offered her the world just because she looked good. They didn't know her, she said, and she didn't know — or care to know — them, and yet they offered her just about anything she wanted if she agreed to consider them for marriage.

"Good God, father, is there anyone in the world I can really trust?"

"My daughter, if I could get a big diamond I'd give it to you. You can entirely trust me, and I don't want anything in return. And I don't want to marry you, my princess."

Shortly after he overheard this conversation the unhappy Randy saw an article on the Internet about the discovery of the largest diamond ever found on the North American continent. A rough stone the size of a hen's egg, it had a yellow cast and was found in northern Canada. It was currently on display in Calgary. A vague plan began in Randy Didler's mind. "What if..." he said to himself, during his long, happy days so far away in Venezuela and so near to his beloved Dani.

He thought for many days about this. The plan, originally cloudy in his mind, took vague form. He knew old man Cabello wanted a big diamond to give to his daughter. Why not this one? Lots of people have begun wearing uncut diamonds in suitable settings. What if.... "What if I can give him the stone? What might he give me in return? What's it actually worth to the man?"

Randy was aware the current Maduro-based government in Venezuela was hiding gold, most of it going to Erdogan in Turkey. But the gates were shutting down and it would not be easy for Maduro to get much more gold out; and suddenly, none of it could go to Turkey. The government was also removing and hiding other items, including some of its top personnel. Hell, Randy knew all about that. He was involved in that; that's why he was in the country.

So if he could help Maduro or, more important, his second-in-command Cabello, move significant and expensive stuff to a location other than Turkey, then Randy might also be able to gain something tangible, along with getting in Dani's good graces. Something like a good double handful of all that gold.

Randy needed help, and he knew someone who might be able to help. "Lando Canunny's tight with Cabello. He said he used to be Canadian. Maybe if Lando or I give Cabello the big diamond we can get Cabello to send his gold to Canada instead of Turkey, which is closed now. Because we're both CIA, maybe we can pull some strings with our home boys, or our carrier aircraft, and they can get the gold shipped to Canada. Maybe they'll pilfer some of it along the way, but if CIA gets the gold sent in hiding to Canada, that means it's out of the country, safely out of Venezuela. That'd be a feather in the hat of the U.S. and it might help the U.S. deal with Maduro down the line. Also, if CIA sends it to Canada, that might indicate that either CIA or Canada has a claim on it, not Maduro. At the very least it's leverage against the bastard. So it'd be a good thing if we can get it done."

The problem seemed to be how to get the diamond. One night Randy met with Lando after work at one of the local bars. "Lando, I've got a problem I wanna run by you. Strictly top secret, okay?"

"Sure. What gives?"

"Did you hear about that big diamond found in Canada recently?"

"Yes I did. Biggest ever in North America. I've even seen a bunch of pictures of it. Looks like something the boys in our labs could make up in an afternoon."

This information floored Randy. "What? Can CIA make diamonds?"

"Fake ones, sure. So-called 'paste' gems. We do it all the time for clandestine ops. That rough stone wouldn't even need to be cut, which is what takes the most time and skill making up phony jewels."

"Would it be possible to make up an exact copy of that big rough stone and, somehow, swap it for the real one?"

"Randy, making it up is no problem. Swapping it out would be tricky. *Real* tricky. They'll have top security on it. If someone could actually lay hands on it, say, a sleight-of-hand man, then sure, the gem could be obtained. But the diamond company would soon find out they'd been had, and they'd go after whoever last touched the stone."

"Yeah, but I read they're not going to cut that bitch for some long time. They need to examine it, show it around a bunch for publicity, get bids on cutting it, and so on. So a fake might not be discovered for a long time."

"Actually I know a way to get it." Lando drank more beer. "My sister has a TV show on which she interviews people. It's called *Fun For Your Life*. You might've seen it along the way."

"I did. Is Molly Fender your sister?"

"Yeh. My birth name is Fehnder, same as hers before she changed it for TV. Anyway, she can go up there and do an interview about the stone, or with the CEO of the diamond company that found it. Top-notch interest item. Get good publicity for the diamond company. Then she can take along a guy I know who used to be a sleight-of-hand man, but turned to acting some time back. If he can handle the stone, you know, *touch* it, he can swap it for a fake. Be a piece of cake for him."

"So, how do we get our boys at CIA headquarters to make a phony stone?"

"Why should they? What's in it for them?" Lando caught the waitress's eye and ordered two more beers.

"How about twenty tons of gold," said Randy.

"Bahoogus! What?"

"Idea I had. Maduro, or actually Cabello, has some gold he wants to send to Turkey, but can't. He desperately wants to get it out of Venezuela and hide it somewhere. He also desperately wants a big diamond for his daughter, Cabello does. Not sure exactly why. The girl's got pretty much whatever she wants anyway, all the time. But her old man does want to give her a big diamond. So if we give him the biggest diamond on this continent, he might be convinced to ship his gold wherever we tell him to, because he can't get it to Turkey any more."

Lando thought about that for half a glass of beer. Then he said, "Let me ask a few guys tomorrow. See if they'll buy it. Might be just what they've been looking for."

And it was, as Randy now remembered with a grimace, late in the evening in his jail cell. He talked to himself. "They bought it all. Zim, zam, pop! Fake diamond made, identical with the real one. How are we to get it to Canada? Can we get Betty Boop interested in this interview? Okay, she's interested. How do we get the fake diamond to her, or to her sleight-of-hand magic worker? Lando, can you do that? Fly to Calgary and drop it in her hand? Sure, no problem. Where is Lando gonna pick up the fake stone? Denver airport. Someone there will hand it to him if he says the right stuff to identify himself.

"And it all worked. Lando left, flew to Denver, got the stone, flew to Calgary, gave the friggin' stone to Billy-Bob the magic man who deftly switched it for the real thing. Then Billy-Bob and Lando and Betty Boop...what was her name? Molly Fender, that's right. All three of them fly to meet me in the deep woods in Idaho. And bango, they're dead and me and Bledsome and

Marsters have the friggin' stone. But Bledsome and Marsters never touched it, the bastards. It was a good plan the three of us made up after I got Lando to get the damned thing made. We had to cut Lando out of the deal. Bledsome and Marsters would fly me and the stone out of the backwoods, leaving the three guys dead there for the coyotes. We'd take the stone to Cabello, I'd get the girl and we'd all get a big chunk of that gold for helping Cabello get it out of Venezuela. Screw Lando. He had eyes for Dani too, but the fucker never said shit about it.

"Then I outthunk Bledsome and the other guy. I stole that canoe, and avoided getting shot or arrested by whoever was comin' to see about the shots. If I could deliver the stone my own self I'd get the gold and the girl both. Marsters and Bledsome didn't do anything. They didn't kill three people for the deal. I did! But shit! I get back to Mexico City, give the damned stone to Dani, and what the fuck do I get for it? One lousy kiss on the cheek, a stupid 'thank you,' and exiled to that lousy room over the store there. Never even got in her pants.

"Next you know, Marsters and Bledsome drop by to try to take back the stone. I told 'em I always had them in mind, like they're part of the deal. 'Hey guys, Dani has the stone. Let's go to Caracas and collect the money, the gold.' 'No, Randy, we've gotta take the stone personally to Cabello, so we need to get it back from Dani.' How the bastards found me in Mexico I'll never know. So they're runnin' a stakeout on the girl's house there. Idiots! I wasn't even in that house. But they wanted the stone. I told 'em where we'd be, tonight at the concert, so they wouldn't blow the deal with their stupid stakeout. 'We're goin' to the concert tonight. Stop us outside the hall and tell me I'm under arrest, and that'll be a signal for me to disappear.' And Bledsome, the foolish fucker, gets hisself killed by her guards tryin' to take the goddamn stone. So I disappear and then this dude sticks a gun in my ear, and here I am.

"But, by God, Dani's friggin' father, ol' man Cabello, is indebted to me, and I will, by the lord Harry, get my gold for it. I delivered what that asshole wanted right into his daughter's hand, even popped for a gold setting for it. Goddamn jeweler asks me if it's the real one from Canada and I tell him it's a fake. So he sets it, and now Dani's wearing it, right now, tonight, off at that stupid concert. And here I sit rotting in jail.

"There oughta be a law about this shit, I mean...." Randy said that out loud.

His jailer heard him and came back to talk with him. It was a slow night in the big town. "*Señor*, I hear you talking to yourself and maybe you want someone to talk to, eh?"

"Yeah, that might be a good idea. What's your name?"

"I am Miguel Alacrán. What is your name?"

"Miguel, my name is Randy Didler. Any idea what that man and woman want to do with me? I mean, where did that arrest warrant come from? When he nabbed me he said something about it, but I was so pissed at getting caught I didn't pay much attention."

"It was originated in Caracas. They told me there was a warrant out for your arrest in the matter of a theft of an item of great interest to some people in Caracas."

"An item of great interest? In Caracas?" Randy started to laugh. "Hell, that's where I want to go! They're taking me at no expense to myself to the precise place I want to go. That's great!"

"That is good for you then, no?" Miguel pulled up a chair and sat near the cell door.

"Yes. I was afraid they wanted to take me to the 'States. That'd be a bad deal for me. A *really* bad deal."

CARACAS CAPER

Randy and Miguel chatted for an hour, and finally Randy said good night to Miguel and lay down on the bed and slept, secure in the feeling that most of his personal problems would be solved by his going to Venezuela.

CHAPTER 18
Delivery

Saturday morning found Rico and Roxy drinking coffee early in the hotel room, fully sated and fully dressed. Someone knocked on the door. Rico got up, peered through the peephole and opened the door.

"Good morning, *amigo*. What cheer?" Rico greeted his friend Modesto, who came in looking fairly chipper.

"Wotcher yourself. Hi, Roxy."

"Mister Mole. How are things underground?"

"Dark, but interesting. Got any more coffee?"

"Yeah, half the pot, and another on the way with some breakfast rolls." Rico poured Mole a cup. Then he said, "Well?"

Mole half-smiled and said, "Ask me no questions, *et cetera*."

"Ooookay!" said Rico. "Ditto."

"When you bozos get done not talking to each other, what are we gonna do with Randy Didler?" Roxy went to the door when the soft knock of room service told them the rolls were there, opened the door, got the rolls and coffee, closed the door, took her pick of the rolls, brought them to the small table in the room, poured herself more coffee from the fresh pot, sat down, and took a big bite of her roll.

Rico answered. "I suggest we get in touch with Sanchez in Venezuela, let him know we have Didler, and see if we can fly him directly from here to Caracas. Any other suggestions?"

Mole said, "We might get a surprise from Venezuela, because Dani already has the stone, and the guys in VeeZee might not want this guy any more. In fact, that's likely."

"Does Cabello know his daughter has the stone?"

"Yes, I'm quite sure he does."

"Why not call him right now?" Roxy asked. She took another lusty bite of her roll.

"Good idea, Rox," said Rico. "I've got the number here. Let's talk to the hotel manager and get this connection made."

After some serious work by Mole in Spanish on the hotel phone, and after suitable delays, Rico was connected to Raúl Sanchez in Venezuela.

"*Señor* Morgan, how may I serve you today?"

"Mr. Sanchez, we have your man in custody here in Mexico City. The man is Randy Didler, who is responsible for the demise of Lando Canunny in the U.S. Do you still want us to bring him to you in Caracas?"

"Yes, of course. That is what I hired you to do, and what I am waiting for."

"*Bueno*," said Rico. We will take a plane directly from Mexico City to Caracas, assuming we can find an airline that still flies into your troubled country."

"Please try Copa Airlines. They are based in Panamá, and I think you'll find they will fly here, no problems. Or you might try Aeroméxico. If they won't do it, let me know and I'll send a private jet for you."

"Thank you, sir. I will notify you of the arrival time. I'm looking forward to meeting you in person."

"*Bueno. Lo mismo. Adios.*"

Rico deferred to Mole to make the reservations for a flight carrying four people from Mexico City to Caracas, Venezuela.

As Mole spoke on the phone, Roxy said to Rico, "Good thing you asked him about flights. I know American Airlines no longer flies to Venezuela. I'd bet there's no common U.S. carrier that'll still go there. Word out is the country's close to civil war. Some of the goons that Maduro uses are biker gangs that're still true to him. I have no idea why, unless they're paid."

"That's probably it. I saw something about that on Drudge Report a month ago, and it looks like things are getting worse everywhere there, day by day. I wonder how *we're* gonna get paid, and I also wonder why they wanna see Randy there at all. Sanchez didn't mention the stone, and I wasn't about to ask him if he knew Dani has it. But at least we're gonna hopefully be in a position to get our money."

Roxy said, "Unless they throw us in jail. Did Sanchez seem thrilled that we have Randy? Could you tell?"

"Not much, but overall he seemed pleased. I wish I knew the whole story about what Lando did down there. What he set up. What was supposed to happen."

Mole cut in. "Let's go find out. The flight leaves this morning at ten, so we should be able to collect Randy and catch the flight easily enough."

The trio repaired to the jail, collected Randy, and took him to the airport to the Copa counter. They got the tickets and boarded the big Copa-labeled aircraft with their prisoner. Rico could not understand why Randy seemed very much at ease to go along with them. There was no struggle, even a peaceful smile on the man's face. After a six-hour, entirely uneventful flight they found themselves in Caracas. It was, as Mole said, decently warm, at four-thirty local time on that Saturday afternoon.

CARACAS CAPER

The airport was next to the Caribbean Sea. As they approached the city, the pilot came on the intercom with some general information about the city. "Ladies and gentlemen, we are approaching the city of Caracas, Venezuela. Caracas proper, or giving it its full name, Santiago de León de Caracas, is on the northern tip of South America, but is actually slightly inland, surrounded by a coastal mountain bank, which you will see as we come in to land. This will be on the right side of the airplane. There is a famous mountain that rises above the city some nine thousand feet. This is El Avila, and as we come in to land you may be able to see the tiny village perched on top of it. Nearly five million people live in the metro region of the city, and though it has been plagued with blackouts recently, it still manages to remain a vital city and the most important one in the country. We are approaching the coast now. You should be able to see the city briefly in a few minutes. Thank you." He repeated the message in Spanish.

Slowing for a landing, the airplane gave the passengers a brief view of the sprawling city on the airplane's downwind leg, and as it turned base and final and settled onto the runway the city disappeared behind the mountains.

As Rico, Modesto and Roxy marched their prisoner off the big bird and toward the airport's main lounge Modesto commented about crime in the area. "Ya know, my friends, this city has the highest murder rate in the world, not including war zones. The pisser is that about ninety-eight percent of all crimes here go unsolved. So we've got to be really careful here."

"We shall indeed mind our asses," said Rico.

"Amen," was Roxy's comment. "May the good Lord get us into and out of this hell-hole safely, my friends."

"And the sooner the better," Mole said.

When they arrived at the airport lounge the trio and their prisoner were met by six members of the Venezuelan military forces along with a representative from the office of Raúl Sanchez. The army boys all had long guns. They kept them pointed in safe directions, as the visitors were relieved to see.

The man from Sanchez said, "Mr. Morgan I presume?" He picked Rico out of the trio like he knew him as a brother. "I am José Canusí, from the office of Diosdado Cabello. I presume this gentleman here in the handcuffs is the man you were hired to find?"

"Yes, *Señor* Canusí. This is Randy Chancey Didler." Rico introduced Roxy and Modesto and they all shook hands. "Do I understand you are from the office of Raúl Sanchez?"

"That is correct. May we take *Señor* Didler off your hands now?"

"No. I prefer to keep him in my hands until I've seen either Raúl Sanchez or *Señor* Cabello. My deal was made with *Señor* Sanchez, no one else. Can you take us to his office?"

"Yes, Mr. Morgan. We can do that. Please come with me. We have a van to transport everyone and there is plenty of room for you and your associates as well."

Except for the army guys, they all got into an older Chevy van set up like a bus, with seats for a dozen people. The inside of the van smelled of mold. Roxy pointed out a rust hole above the sagging headliner where rain had entered, which, with time, had created a van full of mold. One of the army guys rode in the van with the visitors and their captive. The open windows cut the smell of the mold, but it was still a nasty ride.

The road climbed from the airport over the surrounding mountains along the side of a valley through which a small river ran. It was not long before the stunning vista of Caracas appeared in front of the van. The city rose and fell over the foothills of the main valley. The number of tall buildings and skyscrapers was a surprise to all of them.

"Good God!" said Roxy. I had no idea this place was so huge. It goes on and on!"

"Pretty amazing," agreed Rico. "But with all the power out it looks almost like an abandoned city. Like something dead."

The pall of pollution was not nearly as bad as in most American big cities, largely because not much traffic was moving. Modesto asked about it. "Is it hard to get gasoline here?"

"Not for government people, nor for the police and military, but the average man must ride a bicycle. Or walk."

"That explains the clear air," Rico said.

Roxy was still in awe of the sprawling mass of buildings. "It looks like every inch of land has a huge building on it. Oh, look! What's that?" She pointed at a cluster of small buildings climbing the hillside, stacked together like a child's bricks thrown into a corner.

"That is one of the barrios, *señorita*," replied José. "They are on most of the hillsides around the edge of the city. That is where the less-fortunate citizens of Venezuela live out their lives, such as they are."

"Poor bastards!" Roxy replied.

"*Sí*, they are!" was José's reply. "They are poor and they are bastards. Most of the violent crime in the entire city area takes place in the barrios. Do not worry too much about them, *señorita*. They take care of themselves quite well, mostly at the expense of those who have more than they do."

Rico said softly, so that only Mole and Roxy could hear him, "Ahh, the benefits of socialism!"

"I was wrong!" Roxy said, a few minutes later. "There are parks everywhere. Look at all the trees here and there. Looks like Central Park in New York on steroids."

"But there's no one in them," remarked Rico. "Not a soul walking about, among the greenery. We just passed a golf course and no one was on it. I had no idea, really, this place was in such dire straits."

As the sun settled in the west, blacked-out Caracas took on a somber look. The entire city seemed to be completely abandoned, and for the most part it was. No one could do anything in an office high-rise without electricity, even if they could climb the stairs to the top floors. Elevators, computers, copy machines, telephones, heaters or air conditioners, water faucets, toilets, none of those could work without electrical power to run them. So the people stayed home. Others walked the streets for lack of anything better to do. The smart ones crawled into their respective holes and stayed there, away from looters, bums, police, biker gangs, and all the other dangerous elements of a dead city.

Here and there a light shined in a window, but for a city of this size, it was as if someone was walking through a huge mansion with only a tiny candle to light the way.

The ride from the airport took them through the center of the immense, formerly bustling and formerly colorful city. As they rode through the main portion of Caracas, along the eight-lane thoroughfare through the center of the town, the visitors continued to be both amazed and somewhat depressed. They expected to see signs of squalor and the increasing detritus of a decaying society, which they indeed saw, but they also saw the still-glorious beauty of what would be a stunning city, if the power were on.

Along the way they saw many signs of the country's problems. They saw more of the poor sections, monocolored high-rise apartment buildings perched like mold on the surrounding hillsides, no room to breathe, drive, nor even walk very far, stacks of squalor going on and on up the mountainside. The indigent people were not all that visible. The manner of construction of the business area combined with the driver's chosen route to the political center kept the poor and needy largely out of sight.

They finally arrived at their destination. The driver brought the van up a hill past some important-looking buildings. José informed the visitors they were passing through the financial center of the city. A turn here and there, then down a less-grand street and they pulled up in front of a large gray, stone-and-concrete building.

As the van parked in the front of the building, José Canusí announced, "Here we are, my friends. This building contains one of the main offices of Raúl Sanchez, the man who hired you."

The official-looking building had lights on, thanks to a dedicated generator, as José told them. It looked like it would rather have been a bank, a post office or even a morgue instead of the housing of an office of a politician so close to the second in command of Venezuela's current political scene. As it turned out, it was all of those things. They climbed an imposing staircase in front of the building and entered a long corridor with offices on both sides of the hall. José said, "This is a most useful building. The *policia* have some of their people here, and the official police morgue is in the basement."

The first floor had windowed offices on the let side of the corridor near the front door that housed some of the police forces. As the visitors passed the offices, walking along the wide corridor, they could see police officers through the windows busily engaged in police business, all dressed fit to kill in their crisp uniforms and high boots.

To the right was a small postal-department outlet wherein a few people dropped off letters and parcels with the fond hope the mailed items would actually get to their destination instead of being dropped into the nearest dumpster, which was the far-likelier outcome, given the drastic and rapid ongoing dissolution of much of the country's infrastructure.

Next to the post office, down the hall a short way, was a small outlet room for one of the bigger banks. No one was in the lobby. A single teller sat behind the counter with a forlorn look on his face.

A parallel flight of stairs at the back of the long corridor led downward to the morgue and upward to the offices of Raúl Sanchez and a few other worthies in the government. "*Señores* Maduro and Cabello have their offices in a different building," said José.

Roxy spoke quietly to Rico. "Of course they have stairs. An elevator depends on electricity, and that's an iffy thing in these parts, these days."

Softly so as not to insult anyone, Rico replied, "I did see a door that looked like it could be an elevator, behind the stairs to the right on the first floor. But I'd bet it ain't workin'."

At the top of the stairs another corridor led toward the front of the building. Halfway down the corridor they went into what looked like a reception room. It was nicely and richly carpeted in dark green, with newish, comfortable-looking chairs with decent padding, so a visitor could wait in comfort before he was admitted further into any of the *sancta sanctorum* of political power in Venezuela.

CARACAS CAPER

The corner of the room held a desk with a male receptionist. The receptionist, whose name was Francisco according to a name tag on his desk, wore a white, starched-looking shirt but no sports jacket. Rico thought that the distance from the door to Francisco's desk would give the receptionist time to grab a gun out of a drawer and hide behind the desk if the office were breached by anyone who was not supposed to be there.

José Canusí walked directly to the desk and announced to Francisco in Spanish who the visitors were, that they were there to see Raúl Sanchez, and that they had in custody with them the man Sanchez had hired them to find. Mole translated this quickly for Roxy and Rico.

Francisco the receptionist stood up, and Rico realized the man would not have to get a gun out of the drawer. He was already wearing one. Francisco stared at the three visitors and at the man in the handcuffs for about a minute, examining each in turn, presumably checking for weapons.

"If that's what he was looking for," Rico thought, "he failed. He didn't notice the concealed 380's that Mole and I have in our jacket pockets, nor Roxy's PPK in her waistband rig. Or if he did, he doesn't care."

Roxy noticed Francisco spent quite a lot of time staring hard at her legs, which were on good display below her short dark-blue skirt. She wore black ankle boots with stout heels, the kind that would permit her to run, or deliver a solid kick as the need arose. When she realized the man was giving so much attention to her legs she felt like delivering a solid kick right then. "I'm a trained agent," she said to herself. "That means I can restrain myself from mashing your nuts, mister, at least for the next few minutes. But ten seconds more of ogling and my training goes out the window along with half your groin."

Francisco said something to José Canusí, and left the room through a door to the side of his desk.

"He asked us to wait a minute, Mr. Morgan. Please be seated."

The gang took advantage of the fine, comfortable chairs. Rico removed Randy's handcuffs. There was really no place he could run to, and — a fact that Rico thought somewhat odd — he didn't seem the least bit worried.

Five minutes later the door opened and in walked Francisco the receptionist with two men behind him. Francisco glanced again at Roxy's legs and then announced to the visitors in accented English, "*Señor* Raúl Sanchez and associate to see *Señor* Rico Morgan and company."

Sanchez's associate was the CIA man Jack Marsters.

CHAPTER 19
Sally

The same Friday afternoon that Rico and Roxy apprehended Randy Didler in Mexico City, Sally Foarth's phone rang in Idaho. It was Tom Dickannary, her head of section at NSA.

"Sally, we have a gig for you in Caracas, if you care to go."

"Details please, what's the music and what do you want me to do?"

"It's first violin for a string quartet of Bach's music to be performed for the wedding of one of the luminaries of the Maduro government who wants to get married with honors, while that old regime still holds power...which it begins to look like it may do for a long time, by the way."

"Venezuela is closed to U.S. citizens. How do we get around that?"

"You'll be going in as part of a Mexican group."

"Okay, so what do you want me to do there?"

"We'd like you to gather information about the state, mental state that is, of Maduro, Cabello, Sanchez, any other higher-up members of the old regime to whom you can gain access, and also whatever you can find out by hearsay. See if there's any chance of these higher mucky-ups leaving the country anytime soon. Find out if Maduro might be losing some of his grip on, or control of the military. See if you can assess the intent of the recently arrived Russian troops. Finally, see what gives with the motorcycle gangs that work for Maduro. See if there's a chance of getting them to loosen up and maybe switch to the other side."

"That last might be tough. I'd have to hang out at cheap bars to get to find out anything about them. My Spanish is okay, but I can't talk like a native, and somebody would smell a rat."

"No problem. One of the other quartet members, the second fiddle, name Cassandra Saint John, or Cassie, is also one of ours, and a native Spanish speaker. She used to be Cassie San Juan, born in Mexico. You and she can be buddies there and hang out wherever is necessary."

"What about getting out of there? I hear the government has stopped flights leaving Caracas."

Tom told her, "We will have our own aircraft, disguised as an Aeroméxico airplane, to fly you in, stand by for three days and fly you home. Actually the airplane will go to Colombia for three days while you do your thing, and return specifically for you. You'll arrive one day, play the wedding and the reception maybe into the night of the second day, and fly out on day three. That'll give you two nights at most to check the bars about the bikers. You might pick up other stuff during the wedding, which many of the luminaries are expected to attend. Backing up a bit, we'll have a shuttle at Missoula to take you directly to El Paso, and then the Aeroméxico airplane will take you and the other quartet members directly to Caracas. You'll leave Caracas after three days, as I said. The same Aeroméxico aircraft will be there for your extraction on the third day, and by the way it'll have plenty of backup personnel on board in case things get hairy. Our people on the airplane will be disguised as tourists passing through to Rio, which is next on its 'official' itinerary. You and the other quartet members will get on, the plane will head for Rio and then turn about and head back to El Paso. The shuttle in El Paso, once again ours, will get you back to Missoula, and then a driver will take you home."

"Okay, so I'm to find out the minds of the lefty government masters, switch the bikers to Guaidó, solve the Grand Unified Theory, and figure out Zero-Point Energy. That it?"

"Yep."

"When do I leave?"

"Tomorrow, if you can."

"I need to get some critters cared for. Maybe I can still do that today. I'll let you know if not. What time, and where?"

"Let us know if you can leave tomorrow morning at six a.m. If so, you'll be in Caracas by six p.m. or seven at the latest. We'll have a car pick you up in the morning and get you on a chopper flight to Missoula, then one of our aircraft will get you to El Paso where you'll join the other quartet members, and then you'll all take our phony Aeroméxico flight to Caracas. I'd suggest you take an inexpensive violin. And Sally, thank you."

Sally broke the connection and said, "Shit! I wanted peace and quiet and now I'm going into the friggin' lion's den. 'All we want, Sally, is for you to become Maduro's lover and get him to fly to France and stay there.' Might as well be that. Nothing's ever easy in this business. Maybe I oughta quit NSA and open a restaurant. Or maybe a pool hall."

The various flights took up all Sally's day. The last one, from El Paso to Caracas, was the longest but the most enjoyable. After the uneventful flights from near her home to Missoula and Missoula to El Paso, Sally boarded the 'hijacked' or phony

Aeroméxico flight to Caracas, and on that lengthy flight she got to know Daniel the cellist, Tomás the viola player, and especially the other NSA girl, second violinist Cassandra Saint John.

Like Cassie, Daniel and Tomás were both born in Mexico but were now U.S. citizens. The two men had also been hired by the NSA for this operation but they were not officially part of it. They were fluent in Spanish. Although they were not tasked to learn anything about the political situation in Venezuela, the NSA knew they might hear things there that would be of value. They were both excellent musicians, as was Cassie.

On the long flight, Cassie and Sally hit it off right away.

"How long have you been in on operations like this?" asked Sally.

"For about three years now," said Cassie. "Ever since my divorce."

"Oh. Sorry to hear about that," Sally replied. "How long were you married?"

"Four years. Got hitched when I was twenty-six to a Greek fellow. Nice guy, a scholar I met at college, but my God, was he boring!"

"Scholar at what, if I may ask?"

"Greek mythology, with side interests in paleontology and entomology. You might say he studied old bugs and dead people."

"Good grief!" replied Sally. "What was your interest in college, your major?"

"I was interested in him, 'cause he had great looks. Still has 'em, but he has the sex drive of...of an old bug. But also literature. I studied music, obviously, and also the writings of eighteenth-century authors. Wanted to become a teacher. Got married instead. And divorced. All I teach now is some fiddle, and I'm part of the Denver Philharmonic. Pays a few bucks, enough to keep me off the streets. How about you? You ever married? What'd you learn along the way, or study, or do for fun?"

"No, never married. I studied music obviously, to ditto you. Studied it for many long years now, ever since I was about three. I had a knack for the violin, became a soloist, and began touring here and there. In college I got involved with political science and got to know some people in high places in U.S. government. These higher-up politicians thought I might be able to help them as I toured the world. They approached me one day on campus, back when I was studying not only music and poly sci, but also math and, believe it or not, physical education. I had some training when I was much younger in gymnastics, some dance, and then martial arts. I had a solid background in martial arts by the time I got to college, and wanted to learn more about what the body can do. Hence phys ed studies." Sally didn't tell Cassie she was highly proficient in Jeet Kune Do, the technique of the immortal Bruce Lee.

She continued. "So when NSA approached me some years ago my first question was, 'How much?' They gave me a tentative price suggestion. I told them to double it, they did, and here we are, going to Venezuela to change the world."

"Wow! Martial arts!" Cassie was impressed. "I try to keep fit, because it helps my practicing during long sessions. I practice standing up. But I don't know any martial arts stuff at all. Maybe I should, if these guys keep hiring me. So, can you crack bricks?"

"Yes, but I use a gun!"

They both laughed.

"Well, my friend, what can we hope to find out down there in Caracas?" Cassie asked. "My guys told me to find out if the bikers are solid with Maduro or if they might change allegiance to the other guy."

"Same here. Also I'm supposed to try to find out what the big heads, the top politicos that is, at the wedding feel like about the national situation. Looks like we'll head off to a biker bar as soon as we get there. You ever been to VeeZee before?"

"No. Born in Mexico, and then moved to the U.S. in my earliest teens. Do I still have an accent?"

"Not that I can tell," said Sally. "Why do you ask?"

"There's this guy...."

"Ah, now the truth comes out!" Sally laughed. "Is he on board this airplane?"

"No. He's back in Denver. He may be married for all I know. But I'd like to get to know him. I haven't been on a date in over a year. After my divorce I thought I'd just date around, but it didn't happen. I met a guy, we dated a few months, bang, bang, bang, then goodbye. Then nothing for a year. Same thing happened several times since then, the latest just a few months back. It's been pretty quiet in my life. Then I met this guy in the orchestra, a new guy. Plays bassoon. He seems nice. You have a boyfriend, Sally?"

"Oh, yes. He's a real cowboy type, lives on a small ranch in Idaho, but no cows nor horses. Just cats. He used to have a dog, but she died."

"Does he have a big hat?"

"Er...no. Why?"

"If he did, he'd be all hat and no cattle!"

"Oh, shit!"

They laughed again.

Cassie asked, "Tell me about him."

"He's a sort of private eye. He solves cases for big clients, like governments and such. Doesn't work much, though. Most of the time he just sits on his ass and plays banjo or guitar. He's trying to learn violin but it's gonna be a while before he can come on tours with me. Like never!"

A while later Sally asked Cassie, "You mentioned eighteenth-century authors. Ever come across, or do any reading of the work of Edith Nesbit?"

"Actually I did. She was the inspiration for a whole lot of later authors. She was the first to use magic in a book without changing the place or format, flying to Oz or stuff like that. Nesbit was the inspiration for J.K. Rowling, in fact."

Sally noticed Cassie pronounced it correctly, as in rowing a boat...Row-ling.

Cassie asked, "How in blazes do you know about Edith Nesbit?"

"My boyfriend loves her books. Says it's some of the best writing in the world, not just for kids. He goes on and on about how Edith Nesbit had famous people who also loved her work. H.G. Wells, Rudyard Kipling, and the like. I've read some of her works and agree it's excellent writing."

With good conversation the time passed quickly, and almost too soon the long flight from El Paso to Caracas was over. The quartet members were taken via an ancient airport shuttle bus to their hotel, which had reservations waiting for them, made by NSA under the banner of a common travel agency.

"Let's go get a drink," Cassie suggested, as soon as they were settled into their hotel room. "I saw a busy-looking bar just down the road. I can see it from here," she said, leaning over the balcony of their hotel room. "It even has lights on. But the rest of this burg sure looks dead," she said. "All the buildings are dark."

"That's the power outage," said Sally. It's turning Caracas into a ghost town at night. But yes, let's go hit that biker bar. Might as well go do our job."

The two women made their way through the gloomy dusk to the well-lighted bar. A generator out back throbbed life into the lights of the place. A dozen motorbikes were parked in front of the bar. The crowd was mixed bikers and a variety of rough-looking people, and quite a few respectable-looking Venezuelans out for as fun a Saturday night as booze could give them.

The two girls were singled out by one of the biker boys as soon as they entered the smoky room. He swaggered over to them and said in Spanish, "Hey, babes, I'm Pedro. Why don't you buy me a drink? You look like you can afford it!"

Both girls wore simple clean country-type clothes, the sort of thing a farmer's daughter or maybe a dedicated line-dancer might put on to go to a bar on Saturday night. Pedro looked to be extremely powerfully built and was at least six feet tall. He might have been thirty, wore gray jeans and a loose yellow shirt with open collar. He had a red scarf worn like a do-rag on his head. Unlike most U.S. bikers he wore ordinary street shoes. He had what Cassie later described as, "...a pleasant peasant face with a great smile and white teeth."

To Pedro's delight Cassie said, "Okay! What do you want?"

Somewhat taken aback, Pedro stammered, and finally said, "Buy me a beer!" He really wanted rum or whiskey but was so surprised, a beer was all he could think of.

Cassie and Pedro and Sally sat at a table next to a table-full of obvious biker types. Sally could make out some of their conversations, but none of it made a lot of sense to her. They all seemed somewhat unhappy and she couldn't tell what it was that made them that way. She tried to listen in to Pedro's and Cassie's conversation. Some of it was easy to follow.

Cassie was saying, "Yes, we're here from Mexico for just a few days. We're professional musicians. We came to play at a wedding reception for the daughter of a friend of Raúl Sanchez'. The wedding is tomorrow."

"Raúl Sanchez! He's close to Cabello, isn't he? What's that bastard up to these days?"

"Bastard, eh? You don't like him? I thought you guys all loved the boys at the top of the ladder."

"No, *señorita*, they have all the money right now and have all the power. We play along with him because he gives us money to do so. When the money runs out, we'll back that other guy who's declared himself the head of the state. At least we will if the military guys go with him. We're not stupid. Without the money and the military backing we'd either leave the city or stay hidden, out of sight of all the politicians. So, what kind of music do you play?" He directed this question to Sally.

"Classical," Sally answered. "Bach mostly. We're half of a string quartet. We're the two violinists."

This sort of interchange went on a while. Finally Sally asked Pedro what the guys at the next table were grouching about.

"For one thing, they wonder why you have not invited all of them to come sit with us," said Pedro jokingly. "Seriously, they may be crude bikers but unlike me they are all cowards and gentlemen who will not intrude upon us unless they are asked. And because I am the head of our little gang, I will not ask them!" Pedro laughed. "Sally, since you want to know, and your friend Cassie here also wants to know, we are not at all happy with the current regime. But they pay us well, so...there you have it."

"Are all the biker gangs like yours?" asked Cassie. "And what is the name of your gang?"

"We call ourselves *Los Lobos*. And no, the other gangs are not so polite. They come from out of town, some of them, and from the poorest sections of the barrios. One gang, called *Los Culos*, are vicious. They have no manners. We don't like them and will fight them tooth and nail rather than take any of their *caca*. So you watch out for them, my friends."

The evening went on in a friendly and pleasant manner, but Cassie and Sally knew they had to get back to the hotel soon because of an early day tomorrow. They'd get together early with Daniel and Tomás, the other two members of the quartet, for a practice session before the wedding, which was scheduled for noon the next day.

"Pedro," said Cassie, "thank you and the rest of *Los Lobos* for being such gentlemen this evening. I'm sorry we don't have more time, but after the wedding we'll be leaving the country. I'm going to buy you and your boys a round of drinks as a reward for your polite good manners this evening."

"*Señorita*, thank you so much! It has been my pleasure to sit and talk with the both of you this fine evening. I wish you the very best luck in the future."

Cassie went to the bar, told the man to give the gang whatever they wanted, and paid the tab for all the drinks.

As they left the bar that night, Sally expressed her feelings. "I can't believe what just happened. If these bikers were in the U.S. they'd try to keep us here all night, and those guys at the next table would have been all over us. Maybe some members of the Maduro regime are not all bad."

"It would seem that the average biker is a whole lot more polite here than back home, Sally. But of course, my friend, we're not being exposed to the nitty gritty portion of this part of the world. The great unwashed inhabitants of this huge city are in no position to come into a bar. They have no money. What little money they may have is essentially worthless because of the explosive inflation they've had here. All the poor have is anger and frustration at the current situation. These bikers have Maduro's money so they're above most of the problems. But you're right, this 'biker bar' was a joy compared to anything in the U.S., that's for sure."

Sally replied, "It sure was a fun Saturday night. We might even have learned something!"

CHAPTER 20
Plotting

Earlier that same Saturday evening Rico, Mole and Roxy were meeting with Raúl Sanchez, who had just walked into the room with Jack Marsters, the CIA man, in tow.

"Marsters, what the hell are you doing here?" Rico nearly exploded. "You got your buddy killed in Mexico, you disappear, and now here you are? What the hell!?"

"Morgan, I'm here to collect my buddy Randy and collect our payment from Mr. Sanchez here."

"'Our' payment? What the hell, yet again!?"

"Yes, our payment. We were the ones who got that big rough diamond to Daniela Cabello, and that's exactly what her father wanted. So it's big-time for us, and we thank you for kindly delivering Randy to Venezuela. He didn't even have to buy a ticket." He laughed.

Randy walked over and stood next to Marsters and Sanchez. Rico noticed Sanchez did not have the jolly smile of the other two men, both CIA rogues as they all now knew.

Mole said, "So you two bastards are the ones who killed the three people in Idaho. You shot them to get the stone so you could give it to Daniela and get a chunk of gold in payment, and you did it with the blessing of *Señor* Sanchez here?"

Raúl Sanchez spoke for the first time since he entered the room. He spoke excellent English. "Gentlemen, please. You all will get what's coming to you. Just be a little patient. Greetings, Mr. Morgan. I welcome you and your associates to Caracas." He bowed over Roxy's hand in the manner of an ancient courtier, and then shook Rico's and Mole's hands. He said nothing to Randy Didler and barely acknowledged him.

"I have payment for you, Mr. Morgan, for the delivery of this man to me here. I regret to inform you the payment is in the form of gold, which I think you might find more useful than a big bag full of our useless currency. If I figured correctly, allowing for the advance payment I already wired to your offices, the remainder will be covered by these three one-kilo gold bars. He indicated a box on the desk which he had brought with him. Again I apologize for the inconvenience of this manner of payment, but...." He let his voice trail off.

"No problem at all, sir," said Rico. That's going to be easier to deal with than a huge box of your cash, and I'm sure my compatriots agree. May I ask what you are going to do with Mr. Randy Didler? I'm not sure why you wanted us to bring him. He is wanted in the U.S. for murder. We had to overlook that because it was Venezuela that hired us, not the CIA."

"I cannot say too much about the future of Mr. Didler, but I can tell you that *Señor* Cabello most emphatically wanted to, er, thank him in person for what he did. And because Mr. Marsters was his helper, as was the late Mr. Bledsome, Mr. Marsters is also to be in on the celebration. This will take place after you are gone, or I'd invite you to attend. Perhaps Mr. Didler will visit the U.S. in the future and you can arrest him for the murder charge. But I doubt that. I presume the gold is acceptable to you, then?"

"Yes indeed. That's kind of you sir. I guess that's all we have, then? Anything else that you need from us?"

"No, Mr. Morgan. Good luck with your gold bars and best wishes to you. By the way, you may wish to know you were highly recommended for this job."

"Oh?" Rico was astounded. "May I ask by whom?"

"An old friend of yours from Mexico. You did a job for him some time back. He was, and is, very grateful to you for that help."

"Cordota!" said Roxy.

"Good God!" said Mole.

"Jesus Christ!" said Rico.

Sanchez smiled, turned about, indicated to the two rogue CIA men Didler and Marsters that they should precede him, and the three men left the room.

Rico, Roxy and Mole left the office building and walked down the road half a mile to the hotel that Sanchez had arranged for them. It was a single large room with two bedrooms off that. After dinner at a nearby restaurant that somehow managed to serve them decent food with good lighting in the darkened town, the three visitors gathered in the hotel room as the sun went down. The few remaining night lights of Caracas lit up a few spots here and there in the sprawling city, that Saturday night.

"When do we leave this place?" Roxy was itchy to get back home.

"Monday," answered Mole. "The Copa flight leaves for Mexico City in early afternoon. The only other flight out of here is one on Aeroméxico, also on Monday, that leaves at about the same time. It's supposed to be going to Rio. I suppose if we miss the Copa flight, or if it fails in any way, we could go to Brazil on Aeroméxico with our gold bars, if we can get on it."

"So we've got tonight and tomorrow in Caracas to ourselves," Roxy said. "What shall we do this fine evening? Sit around and play cards?"

"How about we go out on the town," suggested Rico. "We have a Spanish-speaking guide in the form of this natty fellow named Modesto. He can order drinks for us and pay for them with chips off his gold bar. By the way, that's what I propose. Each of you gets one of the gold bars. My group in Boise did precious little to help us down here, so the bulk of the payment goes to those who only stand and wait. They also served. Get it?"

Roxy said, "Just like Spenser waiting at a stakeout, now you're quoting poetry. So, what's your disability dude?"

"My talent is hidden," replied Rico.

"Let's go drinking and stop this ancient jabbering," said Mole.

And they did.

Raúl Sanchez took Randy Didler and Jack Marsters to his private chamber, where they had a drink of decent Scotch.

"What's the plan, my friend?" Randy asked Jack. "We gave the stone to Dani, who by the way blew me off, and now we get the delivery of the gold to, uh, Canada with our own CIA airplane, right?"

"Yeah, that's the plan. We have to meet with Cabello and tell him where and how we want the gold to go. Twenty tons of it, eh?"

"Yeh, quite a pile. Mr. Sanchez, has all this has been considered by Mr. Cabello? Does he know the right way to handle all this?"

"Oh, yes, gentlemen, he knows perfectly well exactly how to handle the situation. You will meet with him in a day or so and then he can thank you personally. Meantime I need to make a phone call. You will make yourselves comfortable in the guest suite upstairs, no? Thank you."

The two men left the room and an armed guard outside the door took them up to a suite of rooms that was both concealed and well protected in the office building. There they found more Scotch, mixers, beer, and a well-stocked selection of easily prepared food and sandwiches. "Well, Jack," said Randy, "they want us to stay put here until Cabello comes. Could be worse, eh?"

"Let's have a beer and some of those sandwiches. There's even a TV and a bunch of movies on DVD's here. Wow! Talk about proper treatment, eh?"

"How much of that gold do you think we can siphon off?" Randy swigged his beer.

"Probably as much as we can carry. Hell, the CIA don't care. It ain't their gold! They're just holding it in Canada until Maduro gets complete control again. He wants some cash out of it to pay off some of his goons, like the biker gangs and some of the other dipshits here who work for him. Then, once he has that young challenger Giddieo, whatever his name is, either mowed down or forced to give up, Maduro can ask for his gold back. He'll never miss a few gold bricks. Payment for our good work, I'd say." Jack turned on the TV.

The men drank and watched movies until sundown, then turned into the beds in separate rooms off the main lounge in the suite. They were very comfortable.

CARACAS CAPER

Out on the town the three friends found what they thought was a happy bar. It had its own generator running so it had lights, while most of the street's other night spots were dark from yet another Caracas blackout. They almost didn't go in because of the dozen motorcycles parked out front. But always up for a challenge, in they went. The found a table and ordered, beer for Rico and Mole, and a glass of red wine for Roxy.

No sooner had the waitress taken their order when one of the bikers in the back of the bar stood up. He swaggered manfully up to their table, leaned on the table, and leered at Roxy. "¡Vamos a chingar, pinche!" Let's fuck! Before he could say anything more, Mole spoke to him in rapid-fire Spanish. The biker stood up, became red in the face and then white, and walked away, back to his buddies at the back of the bar.

"Be ready to leave quickly, my friends," Mole said. "We may get lots of company in the near future."

"What'd you say?" Roxy asked.

"Just a casual thing, not quite a warning. Just a friendly pat on the shoulder among friends. It involved his testicles being shoved up his ass and his dick stuffed down his throat."

Rico slugged down a good bit of his beer. "We might want to drink up quickly. Here they come."

Five of the bikers got up and slowly approached the table where the three sat. Leading the group was the man who had leaned on the table near Roxy.

"Leave the first guy to me," said Roxy, sipping on her wine.

As the bikers got close and began talking their threats in rude Spanish, Roxy slowly pushed back her chair and stood up, facing the first goon. She smiled at him, put her left hand on his chest in a caressing manner and put her other hand on his left arm. Then with a sudden push and pull motion she spun him around. She shoved him toward a nearby table and, still holding his left arm, brought the arm back behind him and shoved up hard on it so the goon bent over. Roxy slammed his face down onto the table, did it again, spun him around, and kneed him forcefully in the groin. The man collapsed, but recovering quickly, put his hand into his open shirt front, reaching for a weapon. Roxy kicked him again in the groin and hit his throat with her other foot as the man pulled out a huge knife. Roxy reached down, retrieved the knife from his now-limp fingers and stood up.

Meanwhile, the other four gang members were engaged with Rico and Mole. Except there was no engagement. Rico and Mole had their Kel-Tec P3AT's out and held the bikers at gunpoint while Roxy was giving the gang leader a lesson in manners.

Roxy drove the knife deeply into the next table with a smashing lunge, reached down for her wine and took a casual sip. "Gentlemen," she addressed Rico and Mole, "I think it's time to leave."

And they did.

CHAPTER 21
Tourists

On the way out of the bar the trio passed a smiling young man who briefly held up his hand. The trio stopped to listen. He wore an unusual green and orange striped shirt that hung outside his dark blue trousers, and a tan U.S. military campaign hat with a floppy brim. He spoke in Spanish, and Mole translated. "*Señores y señorita,* that was a lovely display of force against these hoodlums in this gang. The gang is called *Los Culos.* My friends and I do not like these *culos* and will be happy to go up against them, or take them down, as is fitting, at any time. My name is Adolfo Ruidosa. If you ever need an ally, I am at your service."

Mole told him in Spanish, "Thank you kind sir. One never knows, does one."

As soon as they got out of the bar the trio turned quickly down an adjacent alley. They figured it would not be long before the gang came after them, so they decided to disappear as fast as they could. They ran to the end of the alley, took some twists and turns and soon found the street that led back to their hotel. They managed to avoid the gang and returned to their hotel room for the rest of the night. They ordered beer and wine through room service and made do with that.

"Really, guys," said Rico, "so much of the city is shut down 'cause they have no power, it's kind of a waste of time trying to find open bars. That biker shop was the only open bar with electricity out of, what, half a dozen bars we looked at?" Rico sipped his beer and stood looking out the window at the almost totally blackened city.

Here and there in what Rico could see of Caracas a light glowed from some important edifice. One lighted area was the hospital near the wealthy section. There were a few lights showing on a couple floors of some of the office buildings in the financial district. One or two other unidentifiable areas had lights, and that was it.

Roxy stretched her legs out along the couch, a glass of wine in her hand. "Any ideas what we're gonna do tomorrow? I can't imagine you want to just stay inside."

Mole, sitting in a rocking chair with his attention, like Rico's, out the window, answered. "We might scout the area around where we dropped off Randy. See if there's anything we can learn about the ongoing political struggle, mebbe find out what those two CIA guys are gonna get for a reward."

Rico turned a chair toward the window, sat down and opened another beer. "There's a park near here. We could go there for a while, maybe find some bistro open for lunch. With luck they might not have rotten meat sandwiches."

When Mole went to the bathroom, Roxy stood up and, with her head close to Rico's asked softly, "How are we gonna sleep tonight?"

He replied, "There are two bedrooms. You take the master one and Mole can have the other. I'll stay here on this couch. It's long, it's comfortable, and that way we don't give any positive information about us to Mole."

"You're sure about the couch? I could take it."

"Yes, I'm sure. The big bedroom has a second bathroom, so you can lock the bedroom door on me. On us. If I were in there I'd never lock the door. But you should. There's no need for you to wander about out here during the night. The locked door with me on the couch oughta be proof positive of not much hanky and zero panky between us. At least not tonight." He kissed her and she returned to the couch.

The night passed without a hitch. Roxy locked herself in the master bedroom of the suite with a loud snap of the lock. Mole took the secondary bedroom and Rico slept on the couch. All were comfortable. Although some questions floated in the atmosphere, none of them got asked, not that night nor the next day.

Sunday morning over coffee, scrambled eggs and toast supplied by room service, Rico said, "Boys and girls, it's a fine day. How about we go for a walk in the park. Looks like there's an entrance to it right across the street here."

"Okay," said Mole, "but be sure you've got your *pistolas* with you."

Roxy checked the chamber of her PPK and stuck it back into the holster behind her belt. She wore her blouse outside her belt and it covered the gun nicely. The two men had on their sports jackets with what amounted to pocket holsters for their 380s.

Out they went, into the park across the street. There were few people out. The city-wide blackout had the residents of the city scratching for food and water, the necessities of life, which left the enjoyment of a lovely park to those who did not lack those major resources.

Mole spoke. "I bet the light of day removes people from the streets. With light to see by, most folks can get something done.

At night they can't, so they gather together in the streets and make rude noises that don't help the situation." Modesto Pincata Buena gave this assessment of the empty park and nearly deserted streets as the trio sat on a bench in the abandoned park near noon. They had seen no one in several hours' wandering in the lovely park. Mole lit a Cuban cigar, a Bolivar Mareva, and blew smoke to the deep-blue sky. "The only thing the nightly gathering does is to clarify each person's reasons for his resentment. If they foregathered with their neighbors and were the only one to, say, complain there's no salt, they'd get no sympathy. But if they all clamor for non-existent water, which indeed is the case from what the papers say, then they all have a common ground and a need or reason to foregather each and every evening for reassurance and verification of their personal trauma. They might discover their neighbor has no canned corn. Nor do they. 'Oh, no!' they say, 'there's no corn!' Lo, there's another bit of common ground to let them all complain together. 'We have no water and no corn!' And on and on it goes."

"*Claro, amigo,*" said Rico. And if, by some miracle, corn and water suddenly appear there will be no reason to commiserate together. They will stay home and eat the corn and drink the water."

"What's it going to take to get that here, boys?" Roxy got up and wandered back and forth in front of the bench. "Civil war? Invasion? I mean, if Guaidó were installed tomorrow how long would it take to get this city and this country back to the land of the living?"

"The city and country would start to heal immediately," said Rico. "Other nations, at least fifty that have recognized Guaidó, would send help in many forms. The borders would open up to receive that aid, and in months the country would be in good shape again. Well, maybe not good, but better than it is now."

Roxy said, "I read a brief article in *Russia Today* where some guy went into a grocery store a few weeks back, and found all kinds of food for sale. No empty shelves, he said, as had been reported. Thing is, even if that's true the people don't have enough of the inflated currency to buy anything. Now, that's a report from a Russian source, and it's weeks or months old, so it might be totally inaccurate today. The stores might be empty. But it's obvious the local money has to rebound before the country can get healthy again."

"I think you're right, both of you," said Mole, tapping the back of the bench. "The only problem is that the present regime has a solid hold on the military. They have the *colectivos* to attack anyone who disagrees with the current leader. He sends the biker gangs and other groups of thugs to harass, maim, even kill the complainers. Maduro made damned sure he had money on hand to pay the bikers and other goons to do his bidding." Mole puffed on his cigar for a minute. "But now, consider this: If he can't raise cash by removing his gold from the country in exchange for solid currency like dollars, marks, Turkish lira, euros, and the like, he's soon gonna be completely screwed. Without any jack the bikers won't lift a finger to help him. 'Course, some'll do it for the fun of beating people up, but some of the good people are armed and eventually those who are armed will outnumber the goons beating on people for fun. At that point the situation will be under control again."

Rico commented, "If the bikers won't help him he still has the military, but word is they're getting fed up. Some of them have defected. Others are grumbling."

Roxy sat down again. "So it's mainly a matter of time and a new regime, from what you just said. This is a huge and vital city...or it was, not long ago. The businesses here, especially the foreign ones — I saw some French and German store signs — will somehow come up with a way to continue to do business. If the current regime stays in power the country is doomed, I'm afraid. Where's Maduro get his money, anyway?"

Mole answered. "It's rumored Cabello is in charge of a huge consortium of drug smugglers, cocaine mostly, but nothing's been proven."

Rico added, "Being as this is a socialist country the people are one way or another forced to give their money to the government, which is supposed to distribute it. Apparently the government has not done so. We don't see Maduro starving."

"It could go to civil war," Mole said, "if enough of the right-wingers are armed." He got up and paced back and forth. "Right now is too soon. Maduro has too much power and he'd put down any uprising. The only solution I can see is foreign intervention. But with the Russians here — and word is some Chinese are on the way, and we know Cuba also supports Maduro — foreign intervention might take us into World War Three. Any way you look at it, it's a stinkin' mess."

"Anyone want lunch?" Rico stood up. "I think we're gonna have to go back to the hotel to get it. I didn't see any street vendors, not with the massive food and money shortages."

"How in hell does the hotel manage to have food?" Roxy asked.

Mole explained. "Money. The hotel gets money from visitors, and because they want the money to keep coming they buy food, probably from Colombia or maybe even from the biker gangs or the government. Thus the word gets out that wealthy visitors, such as we three, can find clean rooms and decent food for prices that are more than reasonable to us."

162

CARACAS CAPER

As the trio approached their hotel a solitary motorcycle with two riders rode by. The passenger stared hard at the trio. The motorbike kept on going, down the street.

After lunch the three visitors decided to stay in the hotel room for the early afternoon. Mole took a nap. Rico and Roxy played cards, poker for pennies. Roxy won twenty cents from Rico.

"You cleaned me out, madam. I'm broke! Cain't go home! Need a barrel to cover my nakedness. Woe is me! Stuck in Caracas." Rico complained softly so as not to wake Mole in the next room.

"That sounds like the title of a song. 'Stuck in Caracas.' Marimba, a guitar, soft drums, clarinet, and Bing Crosby on vocals. Maybe a piano."

"No! No piano. They ruin a good song. Unless the singer is Ella Fitzgerald or Nat King Cole."

"Nat King Cole? I thought I was going back a ways with Bing Crosby. We do dwell on the past, don't we!"

"I could have said Grimes, or Billie Eilish, or maybe no singer and just Elliana Walmsley doing an interpretive dance to 'Stuck in Caracas.' How about that? Maybe even Sarah Phoenix, or Alexus Oladi. That modern enough for ya?"

"Rico, do you really think I don't know who Ellie and those others are, and would have to ask you to explain? You can't fool me that easily. Yes, a dance by any of those incredible young women would really be the hot setup for our new song. But I wonder what the song sounds like." Roxy gathered up her twenty-cent winnings and carefully put the pennies into her change purse.

As Roxy gloated over her winnings, Rico said, "I'll have to sing our new song to you after we get home. And after I compose it. And after I learn to compose. And after I learn to sing."

Roxy smiled. "I know you can compose music, cowboy. I heard some of your stuff back at your house when we all were there after we solved the border problems."

"Nuts. That was just riffing on the guitar. I'll have to make a special effort to invent this new tune for us. For everyone." He got up, frowned, looked out the window. "And especially for all the poor bastards who really are 'Stuck in Caracas' and can't afford to leave this city right now.

"I think another walk for the three of us would be great this evening after sundown."

"How about right after dinner?" said Roxy. "The sun sets late so we won't be in total darkness. That'll give us just one more night to, ah, enjoy this place. Then we can catch the plane outa here tomorrow."

"Sounds like a winner," said Mole who had just opened his bedroom door and walked out. "There'll probably be a lot of folks on the streets tonight, being as it's Sunday evening and the miserable ones have had one more day without electricity. They like to complain longest and loudest on Sunday night. You'll see." He stretched and yawned. "What've you guys been up to? That you can tell me about."

"We wrote a song," Roxy said. "It's called 'Stuck in Caracas.' Marimba, clarinet, no lyrics, just a dancing girl."

"How come I didn't hear it?"

"It's not done yet," said Rico and Roxy in unison.

Mole grinned, on that Sunday night, looked out the window and said, "Let's geet."

CHAPTER 22
Wedding

Sunday morning of that same day, the string quartet got together before the wedding in an anteroom of the main hall at the big church, where they went through their repertoire. They played Air from Orchestral Suite No. 3 in D major, Bourrée I and II from Orchestral Suite No. 1, the Rondeau, Sarabande, and Menuet from Orchestral Suite No. 2, and several others by Bach. The wedding couple and their parents preferred Bach to most other composers, so that's what the quartet was going to play, for the most part.

Satisfied with their harmonies in practice, the quartet moved to a space marked off at the side of the church in the main hall. As the wedding gathering began and progressed, the quartet played everything but the bridal march. That grand old musical theme was covered by the huge pipe organ in the church.

After the wedding, they all, married couple, guests, and musicians, took a short walk from the big church to the reception, which was held at the lovely, sprawling house of the bride's father. Many of the top-echelon politicians of the Maduro government gathered at the house to eat, drink, and listen to the outstanding music provided by the string quartet. Most of the guests paid tribute to the newlyweds by bringing them wedding gifts. The old tradition of sealed envelopes with ready cash was not seen much at this wedding because the super-inflation that swept the country would require bushel-baskets for the local cash, not envelopes. The few that were given contained euros or Mexican Pesos.

As the reception progressed the musicians took a break, and during that recess Sally and Cassie mingled with the politicians to see if they could gather any information as to the state of the government, which is what the NSA wanted to know.

"Sally, what have you found out?" Cassie asked after the two had circulated for a quarter hour during a break.

"Pretty much nothing," replied Sally Foarth. "I see there're some Russians just arriving here. All dolled up in their fancy dress uniforms. Probably part of the recent air shipment from Putin. I guess we better get back to playin'. I see Daniel and Tomás are already sitting there waiting for us."

The two went back, sat down, picked up their fiddles, and the quartet launched into a break in their Bach schedule by playing Händel's Hornpipe in D, the so-called Water Music, which was a smashing success with the growing crowd. As they completed the piece Sally looked to her right and saw a familiar face. It was one of the Russian military men. He approached Sally smiling.

"Miss Foarth, it's been a long time. I am so pleased to see you here."

"Hello, Vasily. Yes, it's quite some time since I saw you in Moscow. Two years?"

"Three, I think," answered Vasily Gorochev. He was a colonel in the Russian army. "But then, time flies and it feels like only two. Especially to we older folks. I did so enjoy meeting you after your concert in Moscow. I well recall how gracious you were to attend the reception after your performance. So many musicians never do that."

"Well, I always try to meet with my fans. It keeps them interested, and that means they'll come back next time so I don't have to play to an empty auditorium."

"I doubt that would ever happen, Miss Foarth. But this quartet is from Mexico, is it not? How is it that you are here with them?"

"Ah, Vasily, their first violin got sick and, because I was visiting in Mexico, playing a small concert there, I was asked if I could come here to play this, er, important gig in Caracas. So here I am."

"That is certainly believable. Of course, you could just be a *spy*!" Vasily smiled hugely.

"But Vasily, there's nothing going on here to spy on, is there? Except, of course, the presence of Russian troops in town." I can play at that game too, Sally thought.

The other three members of the quartet had paused to give their first violinist time to speak with the Russian military man, but Daniel the cellist noticed the people in the room getting restless, looking at the musicians and wondering why they were not playing. With a tap or two on the edge of his cello, he got Sally's attention and gestured at the crowd with his head. Sally got the message.

"Vasily, I have a job to do here and I must get back to it," she said. "Perhaps I'll see you later."

"I'll be sure of it," said Vasily. He moved away and the quartet got back to Bach.

The evening progressed, and during the quartet's breaks the young people along with the married couple danced to popular music, but the majority of the guests, particularly the older ones, always came back to enjoying the quieting, soulful sounds of the quartet after some of the jangling pop music of Venezuela and the U.S. Except for two tunes by Billie Eilish broadcast on the room's intercom during the quartet's breaks, most of the modern music was harsh, and barely resembled real music. Or so Sally and Cassie and Daniel and Tomás thought.

Sally was worried. Between two of the Bach pieces she commiserated with her friend. "Cassie, I don't like the fact that Russian guy knew me. He knows I'm from the U.S. and probably suspects I'm not here just as a musician."

"I saw him talking to one of the big-shots during our last song. They were both looking at you."

"Shit. That means they suspect more than I'd hoped they suspect. It might be a good idea if I, er, took sick and got out of here. But that leaves you guys in the lurch."

"We're about ready to pack it up anyway. It's close to eight, nearly sundown already and I've seen some of the older guests slipping out to go home. Why not do one more session and then we'll all get outa here."

"Okay. Let's do it."

They gathered the rest of the quartet and told them what the plan was. They all agreed, as they were all tired from having played many hours all afternoon and evening.

The quartet finished up for the night, packed their instruments and proceeded to leave. As they left, Cassie glanced over her shoulder. "Sally, did you see those four goons coming after us?"

"The guys in cheap suits? Yes I did. I caught some of their muted chatter. Sounded like Russian, at least it did from the two of them in the cheapest suits. What do you think?"

"I think we should disappear as soon as we get outdoors. If they suspect we're spies they might nab us and we'll miss the flight tomorrow."

"If that happens," Sally said, "we'll be stuck in Caracas."

"That sounds like a song title," said Cassie. "Hah! I can hear it now. 'Stuck in Caracas.' Flute, violins, a guitar, maybe a vocal by John Denver."

"He's dead. If you want a dead singer, how about Bing Crosby?"

The two women laughed and, violin cases in hand, made for the front door. The cellist and viola player had already left. As soon as Sally and Cassie hit the street they turned to the north, toward their hotel, which was maybe a half mile away.

"A taxi would be handy now," said Sally, "but they're pretty much dead in this city."

"It sure looks like a ghost town with all the lights off even now, barely at sundown."

The setting sun cast a rosy-orange glow over Caracas.

CHAPTER 23
Bikers

A bit earlier that Sunday evening Rico, Roxy and Modesto went to 'geet,' go eat, at the modest in-hotel restaurant in the lobby. Dinner was rice and beans with various sauces with some added chicken. Despite being simple fare, they all liked it.

"This is great," said Rico. "I've gotta do stuff like this at home. Costs zip, yet it's healthy."

"How do they get beer here," Roxy wondered. "Is it brewed locally?"

"Yes," replied Mole. "For a while the local brewery, Polar I think it's called, couldn't get raw materials for brewing, but that's been solved. Local beer's cheap compared to anything imported. Tastes just fine t' me."

After dinner that Sunday, their last night in Caracas, the trio decided to walk a mile toward the east, see where that got them, then south a while, then, avoiding the bar where they had the fight the previous night, head back north and then west back to the hotel. The vestiges of good light still lingered in the valley.

"Rico, this is like a military plan," said Roxy. "I don't mind, but it takes the spontaneity out of the experience."

"We don't really need any spontaneity," said Rico. "We just want to get outa here alive. That means being careful to avoid those murderous bastards in the bar. Especially the one you beat on."

"And his friends," said Mole.

None of them noticed the two rough-dressed men across from the hotel entrance as they left for their evening walk. The two men faded into the shadows and, when the trio disappeared toward the east, the men made a fast walk to the bar where Roxy had kicked in the spokes of the leader of *Los Culos*.

Rico and Roxy and Modesto walked half a mile to the east, checking out the activity of the dusky city along the way.

Rico pointed to the big avenue ahead of them. "I see a lot of cars on yonder big street leaving town. I guess they don't want to be wandering the streets of this town when night falls. It'll turn into a ghost town." He shrugged off a chill in his bones and checked to make sure his gun was there. "How soon do the vampires come out of the darkness, d'ya think?"

"Right about now, I'd say," said Mole. "Look!" He pointed down the street behind them, where a group of a dozen motorcycles were slowly coming their way. Each bike had two riders, some of them wearing what looked like ancient military helmets, a few with football helmets, many of them bare-headed.

"Let's get outa here," said Rico. Looking around he saw an alley up the street with a couple men standing in front of it. "Can we make that alley?"

Behind them came a shout. The bikes got louder as the gang spotted their prey and came for them.

"Run!" said Roxy.

They ran.

The sound of the bikes increased as the riders saw the trio racing away from them, hares from the hounds. Another shout went up from the gang.

As they approached the alley one of the two men standing near it shouted at them, pointing across the street. The man wore an unusual green and orange striped shirt, dark blue trousers, and a soft-brim U.S. style military fatigue hat. He ran across the street, leading the way into another alley that opened onto the main street.

Rico slowed down, undecided which alley to take. The street they were on was narrow, so crossing it wouldn't slow them down much in their escape run. "What's he say, Mole?" he shouted.

"That's Adolfo Ruidosa, the guy we met when we left the bar last night. Told us he'd help us. He says to follow him."

"Let's go with him then." The three visitors ran across the street and down the alley after Adolfo. The roar of the motorcycles increased with every second. There didn't seem to be many places to hide down the narrow alley but, Rico thought, at least the motorcycle gang would be only two or three wide as they came down the alley after them.

Rico, Roxy, Mole and their guide Adolfo raced passed a narrow side entrance to the main alley, where Rico noticed two men standing in the darkness there. As they ran past it Adolfo shouted, "¡Levántalo ahora!" Raise it now! The runners heard a sound behind them like a snap followed by a sound that reminded them of a huge bass-fiddle string struck by a giant. To their surprise Adolfo slowed down, but there was nowhere to hide, no doors to duck into. Adolfo stopped and faced the oncoming roaring motorcycles, three abreast, racing down the alley at top speed behind them. Mole did too, but Rico and Roxy kept on running.

Roxy shouted, "Come on, Mole!"

Mole said, "Look!"

Rico and Roxy slowed and looked over their shoulders just in time to see the disaster. The three motorcycles in the lead kept going, but all six of the riders were knocked completely off their mounts. Two of the bikers' heads flew into the air and smacked down onto the moldy dirt of the alley floor. The second tier of riders slowed slightly, but all three bikes were cleared of their riders as swiftly and efficiently as were the first three. The remaining bikes slowed, skidded, crashed into the bodies and bikes on the ground and piled up, creating a massive mound of hot machinery, dead and wounded bikers, blood, and massive confusion on the ground.

"Jesus H. Christ!" said Rico. Though stunned by the dark scene in the alley, he had the presence of mind to swat the handlebars of two of the still speeding, riderless motorcycles that had belonged to the first line of the biker gang, as the bikes rolled by him, one on either side. This upset their balance and they crashed to the ground behind him. The third bike sped past him, riderless, down the alley. Two of the bikers in the last group to enter the alley avoided the carnage, turned their bikes around and sped off, out of the alley and down the street.

"Trip wire," said Roxy. She walked up to the steel cable stretched across the alley. It was secured to a ring set in concrete on one side, and to a stout lever system on the other. It was a tight as a violin string, and about an eighth of an inch in diameter. "Aircraft control cable," said Rico, handling the wire. "We replaced some in my Citabria back in Salmon a few years ago. What a dirty trick to play on these poor fuckers."

Mole put his hand on Rico's shoulder. "*Amigo*, these bastards were all armed and...." He stopped talking, pulled his 380 out of his pocket and cut loose at one of the bikers on the ground.

The man twitched and lay still, and his pistol fell out of his hand. "He was about to shoot you, my friend."

"Let us get the living shit out of here before every cop in town shows up." Roxy said.

"They won't," said Rico and Mole in unison. Rico said, "Crime in this town is nothing they can deal with, with any kind of success. The remaining living bikers in this mess'll sort things out, try to find out who set this trap, and try to get even. But I bet they never find out."

Adolfo walked up to the trio as they looked over the carnage. A few of the bikers were slowly getting up. They began to feel their hurts, broken bones and cuts, and their complaints and moans began to fill the alley. "*Amigos*, I think it best we all get out of this alley before any more of these *culos* get the idea to take things up with us. Come! Let's run!"

"Hold on, Adolfo," said Rico. "Let's see if we can ride outa here. Come on, Mole!"

He and Mole went to the two crashed bikes that had first come down the alley. The third motorbike had continued far down the alley until it ran into a dumpster and finally stopped.

Rico and Mole each picked up one of the two bikes Rico had swatted. Rico fired his up. "This one's okay. How about yours?" asked Rico.

Mole kicked the other motorbike into life. "Seems to be okay. Let's ride, boys and girls!"

Roxy got on behind Rico, and Adolfo behind Mole, and they went down the alley in the direction they had been running. The two men who had thrown the lever to set the wire were long gone. The tightly strung cable remained in place along with five dead men and several others with bad cuts and broken bones lying in a pool of blood mixed with leaking gasoline and broken motorcycles.

CARACAS CAPER

They let Adolfo off a mile from the scene, on a hilltop overlooking the city. Rico gave him a wad of Mexican pesos, about a hundred dollars worth, which Adolfo accepted. "*Amigos*," he said, "things could have been much worse. The *hombres* that set up that wire told me they were going to jump out and kill all the bikers on the ground with their machetes. But instead, they ran off."

"Probably just as well," said Mole. They might've got themselves killed in the process. The guy I shot was not the only one with a gun. Thank you, Adolfo, for your work this evening. We wish you the best of luck in your future. Oh, and lose that shirt or they'll find you."

As Adolfo faded into the night, the trio saw the rosy-orange glow the setting sun cast over the magical valley that was Caracas. The sun still touched the tip of El Avila, but below that the city got darker quickly with the suddenness of the dying sun so near the equator. The shadows rose up the mountainside with alarming rapidity, eclipsed the top of El Avila, and the city was within the night.

CHAPTER 24
War

Sally and Cassie, carrying their violins down the street after the wedding reception had not gone half a block when two things happened. The four men, two Russians and two locals, who followed the girls out of the reception hall caught up with them. One of the Russians grabbed Sally's arm to stop her.

At the same time a motorcycle bearing a single rider rode slowly down the street toward the group of two women and four men. The rider of the motorcycle was Pedro, the leader of *Los Lobos*, whom the two women had met the preceding night. Pedro recognized the two women immediately. When he saw the man grab Sally he pulled his bike over to the kerb, parked it, turned off the engine, and walked slowly toward the goon who had his hand on Sally's arm. Pedro did this calmly, as though he were savoring a glass of fine cognac with a good cigar and good friends at sundown. He took a sap out of his back pocket.

As he approached the two struggling women — another of the Russian goons had his hands on Cassie — he saw Sally drop her violin case, heard her shout and saw the blur of her hand as it drove into the solar plexus of the Russian goon who had his hand on her arm. He let go of Sally's arm, doubled over unable to breathe momentarily, and then Sally's high-velocity foot from her spinning kick caught the man on the side of the head. He fell to the ground. The other Russian with his hands on Cassie looked to see what was going on, and at that instant his chin met the backhand-driven sap in the hands of Pedro. The Russian collapsed instantly. The two still-conscious men, Venezuelans, backed away with their eyes bugging out and their mouths wide open. They turned about and ran back toward the house where the reception had been given.

Pedro said to Cassie in perfect English, "Forgive me for intruding but I didn't want your friend Sally here to risk hurting her hand again on your goon. It might have harmed her violin fingers."

Sally's Russian goon sat up, groggy but slowly recovering, and after a few shakes of his head to clear it, pulled a small radio out of his pocket. He spoke a few words into it before Pedro kicked the radio out of his hand. The Russian smiled as he sat on the ground, and in broken English said, "Too late! They're coming."

"Here, *culo!*" Pedro kicked again and caught the man on the side of the face, knocking him flat. Pedro then walked to his motorcycle and got a small radio out of a pocket on the bike, and spoke into it in rapid Spanish. Then he turned to the two women and said, again in perfect English, "Ladies, I suggest you get out of here. There's going to be a war. My gang, *Los Lobos*, are coming now to see what these Russian 'advisers' are made of. That guy on the ground just alerted his troops, and there may be shooting."

Sally grabbed her violin off the ground, put her hand on Cassie's arm and the two women ran rapidly up the street. They had not gone fifty yards when the sound of many motorcycles shook the night air. Sally looked over her shoulder back to the spot where Pedro still stood over the two men on the ground. A hundred yards behind Pedro she saw a group of twenty or more men, soldiers, pouring out of the wedding house, all wearing Russian uniforms, and all carrying weapons. One of them pointed at the two girls with their violin cases and shouted. The Russian troops broke into a run after Sally and Cassie.

Up ahead of the women, coming toward them, were ten or twelve motorcycles. Fifty yards behind those were another dozen. Each motorcycle had two riders, all wearing helmets, and all the passengers were carrying some sort of weapon. Some had what appeared to be swords or pikes, many had rifles or carbines, and some had handguns. A mighty shout went up from the bikers that rose above the roar of their machines.

Sally glanced behind her again as she ran and saw the first cluster of three Russian soldiers gaining on them, but behind them the remainder slowed to a walk as soon as they saw the oncoming motorcyclists. "Jesus!" Sally shouted to Cassie, "I hope no one opens fire. It'll be a blood bath!"

A shot rang out. Then a couple more. Suddenly the street was filled with the sound of gunfire.

"What the hell's that?" asked Roxy, riding behind Rico on the borrowed motorcycle as they made their way back to the hotel. "Gunfire?! Now?"

"Yeh, not far away either." Rico pulled over to the kerb to listen to what sounded like a raging gun battle in the near distance of the darkened city. Mixed in with the gunfire noise was the roar of many motorcycles.

Mole rode up to Rico's halted motorcycle and said, "War? Street gangs? Whadda ya theenk, *amigo*?"

"Sounds like a war. Maybe some of the opposition is complaining about the service in this fair city. Shit, Mole, that's the way we wanted to go. That second street over that way to the east, through this alley, leads up to our hotel. The street here that we're on ends up ahead so we *have* to cut through to the right, east, then go one more street east to get to the proper street, and then head north to the hotel. You think we should walk it from here? Sneak on back?"

"Hell, no! We might need all the speed we can get to stay outa danger. I vote we keep the bikes."

"Let's cut down this alley here. We can go slowly and if anything comes our way we can spin around and get back out."

Roxy said, "Or we could head the opposite direction and take our chances on finding a better way back to our hotel."

"It's pretty dark back that way, and I don't know if we can find our way to the hotel if we get into the narrower streets by the barrio. If we get lost or run outa gas we don't want to be walking around there in the night."

Roxy looked over toward the darker area in the opposite direction from which the alley led, and saw how close they were to the hillside up which the stacked and packed residences of the barrio climbed in threatening and darkened tiers up and away from the relatively open main city. Roxy gave a shudder and said, "Okay, let's go down the alley."

The two motorcycles poked their noses into the long, dark alley and proceeded along at no more than a walking pace.

Sally and Cassie ran hard, the sounds of a street war behind them. A shot sang past the two violinists, whanged into a wall in the curving street in front of them and whined away in the night.

Sally ducked her head and ran harder, pulling Cassie with her. She saw an alley ahead, on the left side of the street up which they ran. "Down here!" she cried at Cassie. The two women, fiddle cases in tow, streaked into the alley, and then slowed to a walk, nearly out of breath.

"We're out of the gunfire here," Cassie said. I hope those guys behind us didn't follow us."

"They were back a way, so maybe we can get through this long alley before they can get to it and come after us. And the Russians might get shot by the biker gang before they get to us. Let's move faster." The two women, thanking themselves mentally for being in good condition, started running again down the long alley.

They were not halfway through the alley when Sally looked behind them. "Oh, shit!" she said. Here comes one of the bastards! He's got a rifle." The two ran on down the alley. Behind them the lone man ran doggedly after them.

"Oh no!" Cassie shouted. "What now? More bikers?" She pointed ahead down the alley. At the far end of the long passageway two motorcycles entered the alley and came slowly toward the women.

Sally replied, "Let's hope they're part of Pedro's gang!" The two women kept running toward the oncoming pair of motorcycles.

"What the heck?" Rico said as he saw the two women legging it toward them as they rode slowly down the alley. Behind them an armed man slowly gained on the two women.

"Help!" shouted Sally.

"¡Por favor!" shouted Cassie.

"Jesus Christ!" shouted Modesto.

"Holy fuck!" shouted Roxy.

"Hang on!" shouted Rico. With Roxy hanging grimly onto him in the passenger seat Rico gunned the motorbike hard down the alley and flew past the two running women, aiming the motorbike at the lone gunman. The man lifted his rifle to shoot. Rico lifted his hand off the throttle to get his gun but before he could touch it two shots rang out in rapid succession just below his right elbow. The rifleman threw up his hands to the sky, his rifle went flying, and he fell to the ground just as Rico and Roxy flashed by him. Rico slammed on the brakes, wheeled the motorcycle around in the narrow alley, and headed back toward Mole, who had stopped and was talking with the two women.

Rico pulled up, and as soon as he stopped Roxy was off the bike, holstering her deadly pistol. She made a beeline for the women and threw her arms around Sally. "I knew it was you," Roxy said. "What in God's green earth are you doing here?"

"I could ask you the exact same thing!" replied Sally. "This is my friend Cassie. Cassie, Roxy. We're here to play a wedding."

Rico shut off the bike and came to greet the two women. He embraced Sally and they exchanged a brief kiss. "Boys and girls, let's get out of here, please," he said. This is a war zone." The sound of an occasional shot still came to them down the long alley from the battle zone. "I don't think we want to continue in that direction. Sally, who was after you?"

"Russian soldiers from a wedding reception at which we had been playing. There were a whole lot more Russian soldiers on the way, but a motorcycle gang seemed to have come to our rescue and stopped 'em."

Cassie cut in. "Our friends in the biker gang saved us. The gang leader called in his troops when the Russians sent their guys after us."

"Now there's a switch!" said Mole. "Come on, guys. Let's get outa here." He took Cassie up on the seat behind him. Rico managed to put both Roxy and Sally on the bike with him, and though it was uncomfortable for all of them, they managed to ride.

Mole took the lead, riding back the way they came before they entered the alley. He took them to the south a mile, then over three streets east, back north many blocks, then west to the street with the hotel, which they approached from the north, thus avoiding the war zone. He stopped a quarter mile before they got to the hotel.

"I suggest we abandon our rides here and sneak back on foot. Ladies, is this hotel okay for you? Or do you need to go to your own rooms?"

Sally replied, "Mr. Mole, that *is* our hotel! We just never saw nor suspected you guys were in it."

"I guess that makes sense," said Rico.

Roxy finished his thought. "Sure! How many hotels are gonna be livable in this burg anyway."

"Okay," replied Mole. Let's get to our room and we can discuss all this."

And so they did.

The two motorbikes left parked at the kerb disappeared before the morning sun lit up Caracas.

CHAPTER 25
Rewards

Late that Sunday night they all gathered in the big room shared by Rico, Modesto and Roxy, and explanations were the order of the night. They managed to wangle some beer out of the hotel's room service. Cassie made a phone call to Tomás, the viola player of the quartet, to let him know she and Sally were all right. Over a whole lot of beer the five people told their stories to each other.

The violinists tried to keep the fact that they were there courtesy of the NSA from the others. Sally and Cassie went with Sally's cover that Sally was in Mexico playing a small concert, and tagged along when the quartet's regular first violinist got sick. Neither Mole nor Rico believed all that, but they said nothing. After all, they had secrets of their own.

Most amazing to them all was the stunning differences in the two biker gangs. Sally remarked, "Unbelievable there could be so much difference in two biker gangs. You guys wipe out one gang, and the next one saves our asses."

Rico replied, "'Twas not us who wiped out that gang. 'Twas a bunch of disgruntled local boys. As to the difference in gangs, it all comes down to leadership."

"*¡Claro!*" said Modesto. "In fact that's what'll save or destroy Venezuela. In the long run it all comes down to leadership."

"So," said Rico, after most of the explanations were over and enough beer had been consumed, "Sally and Cassie, do you want to sleep here in that big bedroom with Roxy? Or would you rather go back to your own rooms for the night? And by the way, should we ride along with you tomorrow, or take our own bird when and if it comes?"

Cassie spoke first. "I'd just as soon stay here next to you guys. At least you have guns. All we have are fiddles and bows. Now, if we had buttons and bows we might have Bob Hope too. But he's not much help in a crisis." She and Sally giggled. The beer was doing its job on them all.

"Okay, I vote for staying here," said Sally. "We can pick up our stuff from our rooms tomorrow morning on the way out. As to which airplane to take, I suggest we all take the first one that arrives. Either your Culo or our Air-Mexico-et-al, whatever they're called."

"That's Copa, not Culo," explained Mole. "And it's Aeroméxico, not what you said. You might want to get on the correct airline if you want to get home. Now, our Copa Airlines is a scheduled international flight, and it'll go back to Mexico City. I guess the other one is international too, but it's supposed to go to Rio, not back to Mexico or the U.S."

"Actually, it's a hijacked flight, bought off by some friends of ours," said Cassie. It's going to head for Rio to let the remaining air traffic controllers in Caracas think it's going to Rio, but it'll head directly back to El Paso."

Rico kept quiet at this news, but glanced at Sally out of the corner of his eye. Sally sipped more beer, avoided his eye, and said nothing.

"Okay," said Mole. "I vote for flying with these violinists who have a hijacked airplane. I don't want to go back to Mexico. Rico? Roxy?"

"*Bueno, amigo*," replied Rico. "We fly with Aeroméxico to El Paso."

Roxy replied, "As you guys would say, *¡Claro que sí!* Now Sally and Cassie, let's go have a pajama party in my room and let these two goons sit here and grumble at each other."

"Goons?!" said Rico and Mole in unison, looking at each other.

Rico slept on the couch again and Mole was in the second bedroom. As Rico lay there, he heard excess and prolonged giggling filtering out of the big master bedroom where the three women were. This went on for awhile, and then everyone fell silent.

The next morning over coffee, more questions came up.

"Rico," Sally asked, "what about those two guys you brought here to Cabello. Didler and Jackoff. What happens to them?"

"It's Jack Marsters, not Jackoff. All we know is what we were told by Raúl Sanchez, Cabello's aide. He sez the two of them will meet with Cabello personally for their reward. Those two losers gave that big diamond to Cabello's daughter, and they expect some sort of payoff. They sure worked for it, killing people, abandoning the CIA. You name it, they did it. And their buddy got killed by Dani's guards in Mexico for it too."

Sally replied, "What kind of regime would reward them for that sort of action? Kinda tells you something about the people in control down here, doesn't it?"

Roxy said, "The sooner we get out of Caracas and out of this country the better, as far as I'm concerned."

Sally asked, "What about recovering the diamond?

"We were not hired for that," replied Rico. "It's not even in this country. There's no point taking risks to try to get it back, at this point. We got paid to deliver Randy Didler here. That's the only money we got, and in fact it's in the form of three gold bars. Now that we're leaving on a hijacked airplane it'll be easier getting those chunks of gold, and our guns for that matter, back into the U.S."

"What time does our plane leave?" asked Mole.

"One thirty p.m. local time," said Cassie. "Three hours from now."

"What if they don't let it leave?" asked Rico. "Our activities last night might make the local law somewhat suspicious of outsider folks like us, especially if we try to leave the country the very next day."

Cassie glanced at Sally and said to Rico, "Our airplane is supposed to have, er, reinforcements on it in case there's any trouble getting us out of here." The previous night when Sally and Cassie were briefly alone together in the big bedroom while Roxy was in the kitchen for something, Sally requested that Cassie not give away too much information to Rico and Mole about her involvement with the quartet, because she didn't want Rico and Mole to know she was an NSA agent. Or that Cassie was, too, even if they were both part-timers. Roxy suspected, but wasn't completely sure, that Sally was an agent.

Mole frowned. "Reinforcements? What'd you do, hire bodyguards?"

Sally said, "The people who hired us for this gig wanted to make sure we'd get in and get out. I wouldn't come unless they could guarantee we could get out without any trouble. So yes, they hired bodyguards."

"Must have been some big money behind hiring you," said Modesto. "They even rented a private jetliner with phony markings."

"Yes," said Sally. "The money came from Caracas, actually," she lied. "The wedding people are close to the top of the current government administration and wanted a bang-up quartet for the wedding and reception, for their daughter. They called a previous agent of mine who called me. I had nothing better to do, so here I am."

"Let it alone, *amigo*," said Rico to Modesto. "As long as we get a ride home I'm not going to look the bleedin' gift horse in the wallet."

A few hours later the gang, including the other two members of the quartet, were winging their way home. There had been a slight delay at the airport but the 'reinforcements' had not needed to interfere. As Rico noted, "The local cops are probably still dragging off the bodies from our biker alley and the war on main street between the Russians and the second biker gang."

Half an hour after the airplane took off heading for Rio, it turned around and winged its way to El Paso.

Jack Marsters sat up in bed, about the time the Aeroméxico flight with Rico and friends aboard took off. Sleeping late had become a habit for both he and Randy Didler over the past couple days. He and Randy were drinking a lot, eating a little, and waiting patiently for their reward from Diosdado Cabello. "What woke me?" he wondered. A knock came at the door. "Oh," he said to Randy, who also just woke up. "Someone wants to meet and greet us with gold this fine day. Today's Monday and I bet Cabello got back to his office and wants to say howdy to us. Rise and shine, buddy! Today's our day!"

They opened the door and, sure enough, a representative of Cabello was there. He politely asked the men if they could get dressed and accompany him to a meeting with *Don* Diosdado. They hastened to comply, and then followed the man to a waiting taxi outside.

"This is great!" said Randy Didler. "No cabs anywhere in town, but we get one to go see this bozo for our money."

"We prolly shouldn't call him names," said Jack Marsters. "Our guide in the front seat speaks English, ya know."

"Shit. That's right. Our fine mentor in this event is not a bozo."

The man in the front seat said nothing.

A short drive brought them to yet another fine office building. They followed the guide up to the top floor of the building, riding in one of the few working elevators in the entire nation of Venezuela. Down a long hall with plush red carpeting they walked. At the end of the hall was a single solid door, made of what appeared to be oak. The guide knocked, and they entered the outer office of Diosdado Cabello. A female secretary sat at a large desk to the side of the room. She smiled sweetly at the two men and indicated they should take seats across the room from her. Between the desk and their seats a second door led off the room, deeper into the bowels of the Maduro regime's second in command. The guide who had brought them there left them alone. Randy and Jack sat and waited.

Fifteen minutes later a buzzer sounded on the secretary's desk and she said, in broken English, "Please go in now, gentlemen."

They rose, walked boldly through the door, and were in Cabello's inner office. The man sat behind his desk and motioned for the two visitors to be seated.

"Gentleman," began Cabello. "You are here for your reward. Let us run through exactly what you have done to justify your claim for a reward, eh?"

Randy and Jack settled in their chairs and smiled at Cabello.

"The two of you — formerly the three of you, but one was killed by the bodyguards of my daughter in Mexico — intercepted the man who originated this quest. That man was Lando Canunny. Let us first take a look at Mr. Canunny's position, shall we? Some weeks ago Mr. Canunny came to me through my man Raúl Sanchez with an excellent proposal. Canunny knew I wanted to move a large volume of gold out of the country but could no longer get it to Turkey. He, Canunny, proposed an alternative location. He said he could arrange to move my gold to Canada instead of to Turkey. He asked for a nominal payment, a bit of the gold shipment, in exchange for arranging to get the gold out of Caracas and get it flown to Canada. That was not ideal for me but suitable, because I had the need to raise ready cash to pay off my people here. Do you follow me so far?"

"Yes, sir," replied Randy. Marsters nodded his head, with a 'get on with it, old man' unspoken look of irritation on his face.

"I told Mr. Canunny I had to have one thing from him in exchange for my moving the gold at his suggestion to Canada. You understand, Canada had sanctioned me so I could not just opt to ship the gold there. It was ideal, but impossible for me. If he could do this, it would be a great benefit for me and for this country. So in exchange for giving Mr. Canunny a large payment in gold, I asked for one thing from him. A fair trade, you see.

"I wanted to give my daughter a large diamond. I had personal reasons for so doing, never mind what they were. But I promised her I would do so. I jokingly suggested to Canunny that he get me the just-discovered large rough diamond, the largest stone ever mined in North America, from the Canadian company that found it. It would be suitable to cement our deal. To my amazement Mr. Canunny told me he thought he could indeed get that diamond for me. Imagine my joy! Imagine my excitement! To give that huge rough diamond to my daughter...that would be *something*, eh? I made it clear to Lando Canunny the stone was to come to me, because I wanted to personally give it to my daughter. Are you still following me, gentlemen?"

"Yes, sir," Randy said again."

"Yeah," replied Marsters. "You wanted to get the stone to your daughter. We follow you."

"No, Mr. Marsters, you do not follow me at all. I will make it clearer to you."

Jack Marsters' face lost its smirk. He was beginning to understand.

"So, to continue, Mr. Canunny made some arrangements with his CIA cohorts, and then he left Caracas on the same airplane with my daughter. They were close friends, which is one more reason I trusted Mr. Canunny. My daughter was quite fond of him. They flew together to Mexico City, and there they parted ways. Canunny continued his journey, all the way to Canada. In Canada, in collusion with first the CIA as I mentioned, and then with his sister and a mutual friend, they got their hands on the huge rough diamond. How they did this I am not sure, but they in fact did so. Mr. Canunny made arrangements with three other men, named Randy Didler, Jack Marsters, and Billy Bledsome, to pick him up at a remote location in western Idaho and fly Canunny and the stone back to me here in Caracas.

CARACAS CAPER

"Instead of keeping to the plan you, Randy Chancey Didler, murdered the three people in the back woods of Idaho. You killed Lando Canunny, his sister Molly Fender, and their associate Jimmy Fleetwing. You left them in the woods and tried to double-cross your friends by stealing a canoe and making your way back to Caracas with the stone. You got to Mexico City where you tried to get into the good graces of my daughter by giving her the large uncut diamond. She told me she had no use for you, because she thought you were, in her words, loathsome. Your CIA associates Bledsome and Mr. Marsters here found you in Mexico City, where you got back in their good graces by telling them I had a grand reward in gold for you all, for your kind services. It was for that gold alone that you killed the three people in Idaho.

"My daughter Daniela took the stone from you gladly, because after all it's worth millions of your dollars. She immediately informed me she had it, and she passed along some of the details you told her about how you got it. Over the next few weeks I learned for myself most of the missing details of just exactly how you got it before you gave it to her. How am I doing, gentlemen?"

"You pretty much have it, sir. I'm sorry I killed those guys but they were just in the way of getting the stone to your daughter the fastest way possible. Canunny had this scheme...."

"Never mind his goddamned scheme!" Cabello roared at Didler. "He was my man! You are not!" Cabello stood up and glared down at the two men.

"You believe that because you successfully stole the big Canadian diamond and delivered it to my daughter that you should be rewarded. I promise you that you shall be rewarded. However, you must know that my original deal was with the man named Lando Canunny, who was to have brought the stone here to me in Caracas. I repeat, *here to me*!

"Canunny was a CIA man, like you two were. I doubt the CIA would ever do anything with you in the future except hang you if you ever set foot back in the United States. But that's neither here nor there.

"After Mr. Canunny brought me the stone, you see, I could then give it to my daughter personally. Only in that way could the gift of the stone to my daughter come directly from me. That is what I wanted, and that is what Mr. Canunny was prepared to give me. As I said, in exchange for that service he was going to get a share of the gold we would deliver to Canada. Because you killed him you killed the gold transfer. The gold will stay where it is now."

The two men sat somewhat restlessly now, unsure of themselves for the first time since they arrived in Caracas.

"I never wanted my daughter to get a gift of that diamond from you two, nor from anyone else on earth except directly from me. Do you understand that? You murdered Mr. Canunny, and along with him you also murdered most of your chances of ever seeing any of the gold. I say most, because I *will* give you a reward. You *will* see the gold, and in fact can carry as much of it away as you are able to carry. I am sorry things went the way they have. My daughter now has the big diamond, but she does not know, really know in her heart, that I arranged for her to have it. I can tell her, but what does a young girl believe?

"She has the stone, that is done, and she will have it forever. As I said, perhaps too many times already, I am sorry I was unable to present her with that magnificent gift. But she does have it. Also, as I said already, most of your chances of seeing the gold were shattered by your incredible stupidity and blundering in this matter. But because you delivered what she wanted, I will provide you with your reward."

He pushed a button on the side of his desk. A door behind him opened and a burly man strode into the office.

Diosdado spoke. "Take these two men with you and show them the gold, as I already arranged with you. Let them take whatever they can carry."

He said no more. The burly man indicated the door through which he had entered the office. Randy Didler and Jack Marsters passed through it, the burly man followed them, and Diosdado Cabello was left alone in his office. He stared out the window, with the sad thoughts of an old man running through his head.

It began to rain in Caracas.

CHAPTER 26
Home

After a long flight from Caracas to El Paso and a shorter one from there to Missoula, Montana, followed by a drive in a limo provided by an incognito branch of the NSA, the gang of five, Rico, Roxy, Sally, Modesto and, at Rico's invitation, Cassie Saint John arrived at Rico's home north of Salmon, Idaho. They all decided to gather there for a few days of relaxation instead of breaking up and going their separate ways. Modesto Pincata Buena, the Mole, had a home near Las Cruces. Roxy Roades, the CIA girl, lived in an apartment near Washington, DC. Cassie Saint John, the fiddler/NSA agent, lived in Denver in a rented house. Sally Foarth, the fiddler/NSA agent, and Rico Morgan, the private eye, lived close to each other in Idaho.

For the duration of the visit, Rico and Mole slept at Rico's house and the three women went to Sally's home for the nights they were there. They got together at Rico's small ranch every day to discuss things, drink beer and relax. Occasionally someone got hungry and either Rico or Sally would cook up something. An excellent Mexican restaurant was up the highway from Rico's home and one night they all went there.

Rico and Sally noticed there was a growing attraction between Mole and Cassie. They kept this to themselves, but would be happy for the two of them if anything came of it.

They all had many questions, and it seemed like the decent thing to do to gather at Rico's place, drink beer, smoke cigars, play some music, and relax in the summer sun. Then they could get to the questions.

After a day or two of this relaxation, with all of them sitting outside near an apple tree in Rico's yard soaking up the sun, Sally asked the first serious question. "Rico, do we have enough beer? I could drive to North Fork and get some more...?"

"I think we're okay," he responded. I've got several more cases in the back room. We're a bit low on Scotch, only two big bottles left."

Mole broke in. "Darned cats! Leave 'em alone for a few days and the whiskey's all gone."

Sally replied, "Roxy would you please kick him? I can't quite reach him from here."

"Sorry, Sally, my legs have gone to sleep." Roxy sipped a bit more beer. "Maybe in half an hour I can get up, and then I'll kick him."

They sat on Adirondack chairs, and at an ancient picnic table in Rico's yard.

Cassie asked Mole, "*Señor* Modesto, do you have any children?"

"No, *señorita*, I was never so lucky. How about you?"

"No. I was married for a while but my violin took up my spare time. And I never really wanted to have children. My music career was a higher priority, and kids never happened."

"Married to your music, it sounds like," replied Mole. "Could do worse. I'd love to hear you play. Maybe you and Sally could do a duet, no?"

"I think we could arrange to do that. Sally, can you and I manage to do Bach's Concerto for Two Violins in D Minor? These guys need a treat and I want to hear your Guarneri."

"That sounds like fun. No, Rico, you can't play along! It's a duet. That means only two fiddles."

In short order the two women brought out their violins and soon the familiar sounds of the three-hundred-year-old BWV 1043 rang over the eastern Idaho mountain country. After dinner that night Mole and Rico got out guitar and banjo and, together with Sally's violin, played some old and favorite bluegrass tunes. Cassie played an ancient Irish fiddle tune that Mole knew on guitar. They played long after the sun ducked behind the adjacent mountain range. After the sun hid, the full moon lit up the musicians. But too soon, in that high-altitude mountain country, it got too cold to stay outside.

Later that night, feeling left out of the music field, Roxy said to Rico, "Looks like I'd better learn to play something. I've got an old guitar my father left me, a small Martin, but maybe I oughta learn mandolin to fit in with you guys here. Or maybe washtub bass."

"Whatever you do would be great. You ever sing?"

"Yes. I actually know some of the old bluegrass tunes, like 'Little Darlin' Pal of Mine,' and one or two of the Dillards' tunes you played. But I didn't want to ruin excellent music with crappy singing."

"Now thet jest cain't be done!" said Mole. "We both sing lousy, Rico and me, but thet don't stop us none, nosiree. We kin yodel wit da best of 'em! Rox, you is jest gonna hafter sing, next time we gits to pickin' some, tergither."

Cassie said, "You talk jest persackly like a hibbly!"

"A what?" asked Mole.

"Hibbly. Or as those might say who jest don't know, hillbilly."

More beer was had by all.

On the last day of the visit by Cassie, Mole announced he'd be leaving with Cassie to visit with her at her home in Denver. The two had taken several walks alone in the evenings at Rico's house, and they seemed to be getting ever better acquainted. This proposed visit by him to Cassie's home was, for Rico and Sally, good news. He'd been alone too long, Sally thought, and even though Mole had several girlfriends here and there, none of them were serious, or so he said.

Roxy was leaving the next day too. She managed to get alone with Rico for a few minutes and said, "My friend, once again we have a secret to keep. Can we really keep it?"

"I think we can. What happened in Mexico City, er, stays in Mexico City. Who knows where the road will take us. I may very well never see you again. If that turns out to be the case, we have some excellent memories. That, I think, is what counts. And you have a gold brick!"

"Yes I do! Hooray! But don't forget," Roxy said, "what we did was in the line of work. We had to keep each other's thoughts on the job, not on jumping in the sack together."

"And it worked. So, God bless you, let's just enjoy the memories of the past and keep quiet for the future."

"And we can always look forward with hope," she said.

"¡*Claro que sí!*" said Rico.

After dinner on their last night together Mole posed the first truly serious question that had been asked by any of the five of them. They all sat in Rico's front yard, again at sundown, again with a sufficiency of beer.

"Rico," asked Mole, "why didn't you want to get that diamond back from Daniela Cabello? It is, after all, worth millions of dollars, and it's a stolen item."

Roxy added, "Yes, *amigo*, why didn't that get your attention? I know you could've got shot trying to pull it off her neck, but you just don't seem to care that she had it."

Sally looked at Cassie, and asked for both of them, "You knew Dani had the uncut diamond, and you were close to it, weren't you? Could you have grabbed it safely?"

Rico answered, "Yes, of course I was aware she had it. Mole and I saw it on her neck in Mexico at the concert, but I was never in a position to grab it. Nor did I want to try to gain access to her or to her quarters to try to get it back. There was no point in it. Mole might have been in that position, but he never said what happened the night he disappeared with Dani."

Mole said, "She put the stone into a vault as soon as we got to where she was staying. When we got to her place she excused herself instantly. She had the stone on then, but not when she returned to me. I asked her if it was in a safe place and she told me about the vault. So it was not an option for me to try to get it at all. I also knew her armed guards were there in the house too. And that is all I can tell you."

Rico said, "We could have gone back to Mexico City to try to recover it, but no one was paying us to do so. You might wonder why not." He wore a slight smile, and seemed to have a look of absolute peace on his face.

Roxy said, "Good point. We were there in Mexico City. The diamond company could have hired you to recover the stone. Why didn't they? Don't they know or trust you?"

Rico waited a bit, sipped some beer, and then told them.

"Yes, the diamond company knows and trusts me. Thing is, there was never a need to recover the huge uncut stone because that big chunk of carbon was never out of their hands.

"What!" shouted Mole.

"How could that be?" asked Roxy.

Sally just laughed. "Jeesus!" she said.

Cassie said nothing.

Rico continued. "Jimmy Fleetwing never made the swap. After we were hired, one of my first phone calls, with the help of Yeats at Boise Control to get the man's name and phone number, was to the director of Dominion Diamond Mines in Calgary. I alerted him to the possibility of the theft of the stone by Molly Fender and her brother and her friend, and I asked him to please verify the identity of the diamond in his possession. He proceeded to do so, and it was indeed the real thing. He identified it by means of some tiny markings, visible only under a microscope, that the company put on the original. The markings were there, so he's had the real diamond all the time."

"Sonofabitch!" Mole stood up and walked in circles for a while. "So Dani's wearing the CIA fake!"

"Yup. That's why I didn't care to try to get it back."

"And you couldn't tell me?"

"Why? It didn't change things, and the fewer people who knew it was phony the better. If word had got out, not from you or I but from someone overhearing any comment we may have made, it would have changed all the dynamics drastically. Cabello, Dani, Sanchez, Didler, on and on would have done something entirely different. So I could not risk telling you nor anyone else."

Mole replied, "Yeah, you're right. We would have all acted and said different things all along the way if we knew that was a phony stone."

Roxy chimed in. "Absolutely. I know I'd have maybe never gone to Mexico City in the first place if I knew this was all a charade. Why risk your life trying to catch some bum who stole a piece of glass jewelry?"

"¡*Exactamente!*" said Rico. "I'm glad you all agree with me. Sally and Cassie, your scenario wouldn't have changed a bit if you knew the stone was a fake. All you did was go play a wedding for some bigwig in the Maduro regime."

"I agree," Sally said. "I would not have done anything different if I'd known. Neither Cassie nor I had anything to do with the diamond, nor with Daniela, and so forth."

"I actually have no idea what you're talking about," said Cassie. "I wasn't hired to chase diamonds, just to play Bach at a wedding. Which we did. Extremely well, by the way."

"Mole can fill you in when you get to your home," said Sally.

Roxy had one more question. "Rico, what about the guy who murdered three people here in Idaho? From what you said he and his buddy will get a reward from Cabello, but are we, the U.S. I mean, gonna go after him?"

Rico looked up at the darkening sky, in which a few stars were already visible. A meteorite streaked across the darkness. "I have a sneaking suspicion their reward might not turn out to be exactly what they thought it was gonna be. They messed with Cabello's plans, and things did not go exactly like he wanted. I got that feeling from the brief meeting we had with Sanchez when he paid us off. I think Cabello's unhappy."

Mole agreed. "I think Rico's hit the nail on the head. When those two guys walked out of that office with Sanchez we already had three gold bricks in our hands. If they were gonna get some gold for a payoff, why not just give it to them right there? But Sanchez took them into what looked to me to be custody."

"Yes!" said Rico. "I agree. It looked like they'd been arrested by a jailer with a pleasant smile. And he might be an executioner too, not just a jailer."

Roxy thought about that a while. She concluded, "Well, if the U.S. ever decides to try and get either of those guys outa there to indict 'em for murder, I hope I don't have to go to Caracas again. Not ever!"

"Amen to that!" said Rico Morgan.

━━━━━━━━

Off the coast of Caracas was a sunken ship, a barge-like vessel with a large open space on its deck. On its deck rested crates containing some twenty tons of gold bars. The vessel rested on the bottom of the bay some hundred feet below the surface, and it would rest there until at some point it would again be brought to the surface by means of injecting its built-in floats with compressed air. This would permit the salvage of the gold.

Floating near the gold, held to the deck by means of concrete blocks securely fastened to their ankles, were the bodies of Randy Didler and Jack Marsters, their dead eyes open, staring eternally at the crates of gold. As had been promised, they were free to take away as much gold as they could carry.

RAY ORDORICA

CARACAS CAPER

CREATED BY SHEEP CREEK PUBLISHING, NORTH FORK, IDAHO, USA

RAY ORDORICA

www.ingramcontent.com/pod-product-compliance
Lightning Source LLC
Chambersburg PA
CBHW051504170626
46811CB00002B/647